W9-AQC-351

DeFORD

D e

F O R D

D A V I D S H E T Z L I N E

RANDOM HOUSE  NEW YORK

First Printing

 Published in New York by Random House, Inc., and simultaneously in Toronto, Canada, by Random House of Canada Limited.

Library of Congress Catalog Card Number: 67-22650

Manufactured in the United States of America by The Colonial Press Inc.,
Clinton, Massachusetts

Designed by Carl Weiss

IN MEMORY OF

Richard Fariña, who was killed in the spring of his twenty-ninth year by a motorcycle, Carmel, 1966.

Fariña, Fariña, how goddamn unlike you, Richard, to leave us feeling so suddenly sober and alone.

DeFORD

I

On the corner of Elizabeth and Prince, one block off Bowery, a man shakes his fist at the sky. In a doorway behind him lies his newspaper nest with the warm imprint of his body and a few empty pints scattered about. A piece of the nest clings to his filthy coat as he stands staring at the opposite curb, where a bill lies caught on a storm grating. It is the second time they have tried to lure him over, he thinks. Ten years ago he went across, and the first person he asked for coffee money was someone who had worked under him in the office. He had been recognized and a handful of silver forced on him before he could back off. The memory of it is a cramp behind his eyes. He blinks away the pain, sits on his curb, carefully wedges his legs beneath him and stares at the bill. The morning is still of the very earliest gray, and an eddy of wind faintly redolent of smoked leaves stirs the bill, inch-

ing it nearer the grate. Its corner catches, tips up, almost tumbles, but drifts flat. Now he is sure it is a five-dollar bill, and he leans over his curb edge, moaning. Careful, danger! a policeman is rounding the block from Bowery. The derelict springs to his feet and walks away from his bill, face set so tightly it aches. When the policeman crosses onto his block and stops to study him, he walks deliberately erect, chin tucked in and nods, saying with perfect articulation:

"MEMO:
TO: *All branches*
FROM: *Smith, Elizabeth Street*
D. B. Smith is not an alcoholic, he is a way of life." The policeman allows him to pass, but Smith looks back and watches him bear down on the bill. If only someone had come round the corner—they could have split it—but a policeman. D. B. Smith moans, peering from a doorway as the policeman draws nearer and nearer. Perhaps it is only a dollar bill, he prays wildly.

◇ ◇ ◇

On D. B. Smith's block, two floors above Elizabeth Street, an old man named DeFord lay dying, mind slipping away, body already numbed as he dreamed of an Indian hauling twisted legs up his stairs, left hand clutching an ice pick. On his back DeFord heard and saw the crippled Indian—now on the stairs, now at the door, now in his room—the ice pick raised, dark face pinched with hate. He struggled in his dream's envelope while his heart only quivered, its habit forgotten. He made numbing hands move toward a pill bottle, and almost at once the pain ebbed and he felt his heart's beating, a blinded mule gathering itself to plod its circles again, pumping, pumping.

Although he had not dreamed in years, he wondered if the Indian really had said he would kill him, or was it entirely nightmare? Looking around, he saw his room strewn with clothing, bureau pulled apart, his alarm clock shattered. He knew he was not dreaming. Only a few hours ago the Indian had robbed him of his pension check. Perhaps he did say he would kill him. DeFord reached to his pills again and carefully screwed down the cap, smiling when his hands did not shake. One thing is certain, he thought: Joe Raven has stolen all my money and broken my clock.

Absently DeFord held the broken clock while his mind tugged other things, reluctant to register his looted room, his cheap crude furniture, his window still so unevenly clotted with paint it seemed pressed out of lumps of dough. DeFord knew this room; his eye had registered sloppy mitering, butt-end materials, off-pitch and sink of joints and seams. He was a good carpenter, so his senses would not rest from such things; they were immediate as the smell of damp earth. Still, he had scrubbed his window until the last greasy sheet peeled, leaving not frosted glass, as he expected, but clear. Badly kilned and distorted, it still allowed a view of apartments, scattered boderias and the dark entrances of bloodybuckets. Shelter, food and wine. He looked at the street again: built as quickly as possible of the cheapest material, never to be lived in by those who pounded up the frames and covered all with the lowest grade of brick. Through the wavy glass the street was something abandoned on the bottom of a poorly drained pool, and the early morning was a silt settling over the policeman on the next block and the derelict who crouched in a doorway, staring after him.

Since he had been in the city—and that is because of the hospital, he assured himself—his mind had been slipping, leaping at things as if to—what? Dwell on something better. Yet he knew that was not true. What he wanted to do was to put things together so they fit. There comes a time when a house is complete; even if fine work and finishing remain, the house itself is done. He reached out, and his hand touched his *Carpenter's Manual.* It is too gray to read, he thought, but he let his hand remain.

In 1772 the first DeFord, age three and one-half years, reached the port of New York—the only DeFord to survive passage—to be sold into indenture at public fair. Nevertheless, he arrived a freeman some years later at an upstate settlement called Ithaca. No Ithaca for him, though: he was sniped from his front porch near the close of the War of 1812 by a musket hidden in the forest. No one could even guess who had fired, much less why.

Years later in Philadelphia, DeFord's great-grandfather remembered the day and wrote it into the flyleaf of his *Carpenter's Manual* just below the preamble of his union:

> . . . the object of this Association is to avert, if possible, the desolating evils which must inevitably arise from a depreciation of the intrinsic values of Human Labor; and to establish a just balance of Power, both Mental, Moral, Political and Scientific, among all the various Classes and Individuals which constitute Society at large . . .
>
> My father killed on his porch September 3, 1814. A Man of Peace.

The description also fitted the great-grandfather, who died peacefully after losing his homestead in the depression of 1850.

In 1858 immigration forced DeFord's grandfather west, where he escaped the fourteen-hour day by mortgaging himself to a piece of land in Ohio. He added to the flyleaf the issues of his life:

Bennett	Lyman
Born 1862	Born 1865

Brian	Lyle
Born 1864	Born 1870

But he had not gone far enough west, for he had been drafted into the Union army and returned badly wounded from Vicksburg. He wrote then:

> Fanny Wright, my wife—"Labor must rise against idleness, industry against money, justice against law and privilege."

Fanny Wright had not been his wife, but a contemporary of his father's. It might have been the name his grandmother took during the agitation in Philadelphia years before. Obviously his father had spoken of her often; perhaps he imagined her as his wife. The family was already being forgotten, confused, so lost to the history of their country that a man wounded in one war could not be expected to dissociate himself from the heroes of another.

That seems to be what the youngest son, Lyle, felt, although he too might have been only a man of peace, for he made no corrections, simply adjusted the accounts until there was no one remaining but himself and his son, DeFord.

Bennett Died 1897	Lyman Died 1892 yellow fever Mexico
Brian Lost 1883 in wagon outfit	Cynthia my wife Died 1899 childbirth
	Lyle, Jr., son Born 1899

Then he added:

> Lost my father's farm to mortgage, July 4, 1900.

There had been a Cousin Lucelle back in Ithaca, so DeFord was taken there to grow up by the shores of a large lake while his father tried many kinds of work until it was quite apparent that no matter whose side won, a DeFord always lost. Father and son were forced west again when DeFord was eighteen, but west was a longer haul and it was much more difficult for a man of peace. DeFord's father died of pneumonia from a strike fight in Michigan when the IWW insisted that Great War or no Great War, a man shouldn't have to work more than seventy hours a week.

◇ ◇ ◇

DeFord went as far west as he could, and for over forty years worked as a carpenter. A year ago he had first felt the pain under his ribs, and one day his right arm went suddenly asleep, useless for an afternoon. He became increasingly aware of his heart; at night he'd start awake and have to count its beats into sleep. He was one year older than his century, and no matter how far he had kept from unions and wars, his country had grown not in spite of, but because of them. So when he put up a small house for himself in a little town in Oregon, he found he could live quite comfortably on the money saved from hundreds of buildings he had measured and laid. And, of course, social security.

All this time the father's Cousin Lucelle had hung on in Ithaca, an incredibly poor and ancient woman whom everyone respected, as it was known that in her ancient way she had stored up great wealth in bits and pieces somewhere in her ancient house. DeFord had just settled into his first summer of rest when a terse letter arrived from her neighbor, saying she had died at the age of a hundred and two. Not only hadn't the neighbors found a will, but the city of Ithaca had found no hidden riches. Instead of writing, he decided to return, not out of sentiment but as the only DeFord in the *Carpenter's Manual* who if he had not won, neither had he lost. The last DeFord, returning to where the DeFords had started out at the beginnings of their country, to put a decent stone marker on the grave of the DeFord who had held out the longest.

A few weeks later he was walking with hand-built wooden suitcase, erect and alone across the city's great terminal, to the Oregon train—a lean man in a light plaid shirt, long drill trousers, elkskin work gloves jammed into rear pocket, just about to buy the ticket that would take him back to his last house—when his heart stopped. He went down like a tree.

In the hospital his first thought was: It is what I should have expected. He talked to the doctors, watched their machinery recording his heart's contractions, and saw the breath of hesitation where the stylus squiggled like a grasshopper's leg, loosing its hold on the moving paper. Amidst all the doctor's machinery he felt foolish thinking his heart had a will, a purpose; still, were it ever to hesitate, even for a second, he knew it would stop forever. It did not frighten him; it was the way things were; he had great respect for habit.

"No complaints," he said to the doctor. "I'll take a room for a few weeks to be handy for checkups. When you think I can, I'll want to return to Oregon. You write out everything—about the pills and what I may do and best not."

His surgeon was also an old man, so he did not reply, simply looked at DeFord for a long moment, and just before he shut the door, said, "I'll do that, Mr. DeFord."

And so that September morning DeFord had struggled from the first nightmare he could remember in sixty-six years to a ransacked room and a broken clock, without the pension check he needed to return to his last house. A crippled Indian with an ice pick had taken it and left—a promise? Raven's threat was as indistinct as his dark face, and when DeFord concentrated he could only remember such a mask of senseless hate it brought him upright in bed. "They'll be another in a month. I'll declare this one stolen—no, lost. He forgot to make me sign, perhaps he won't dare forge." He talked aloud to make the mask disappear, then got up to dress, realizing the smashed door-lock was now his greatest threat.

Through the window the sky had no blue yet, and the corner where the derelict mooned seemed to mark the end of the city, the streets beyond half seen, half shadowed. DeFord, in low-top boots and drill trousers, lifted his right leg until the material clung to his thigh, and made a few passes with his straight razor to bring up its edge. When he had shaved, he thought: I'll have to get some kind of work-chore for a few days. As he smoothed his bed he saw the derelict across the street spring alive, shuffle to a doorway and flatten into a shapeless clump of rags as a man in tight slacks and a woman's sleeveless shirt minced around the corner. Wearing pointed shoes—one black, one rancid butter—a tiny bag suspended like a pendant around a long neck, and a discolored yarmulke riding a head of curls, he swiveled opposite DeFord's building. For a moment he offered a pasty oval face to the window, then bobbed into a doorway, where he waited, poking at his dirty hair with the flat of his hand.

As DeFord stepped onto the sidewalk, work gloves in his pocket, a small dirty white dog bolted from a trash can and sat down in front of him on the street. DeFord carefully opened his fingers and patted his pockets. "No stones. No food either. Ha!" He fished out a quarter. "Breakfast. You're still here when I get back, I'll bring you something."

The dog spun, viciously nibbled the thin ridge of his spine, then prickled as a tall man paused in the doorway to point a tightly rolled umbrella at the small of DeFord's back. "Top morning, top morning. We're neighbors, I guess. Name's Tanner. Damn, what a fine day." Tanner descended sniffing, umbrella menacing the sky. "Just the day for an old lawyer to get his teeth into a case. Don't you think? . . . You're right, you're damn right. There's all manner of things open to a young man. In the abstract of course, you see? I mean, in the absolute a young man's no longer young at, say, thirty-five. No longer middle-aged at, say, fifty. But in the abstract a man's young till he's old. Now do I look an old man to you, Mr. ——? . . . DeFord, eh?" His face relaxed, but he jabbed the pavement between his polished shoes. "Heard noise in your room last night, DeFord. Would have come down, but . . . around here, you know—not much to this neighbor business." His eyes met DeFord's. "Would have come down anyway, but there was this damn eel under my bed. Big bastard. A while back I would have taken a stiff one, kicked the slimy. But I'm drying out. Needed another dry night's rest. Then fix up a paying retainer today—you know. No more eels, crabs, jellythings . . . Was it that damn Raven?" DeFord nodded. Tanner looked away. "Took me for a few dollars. Just before I got here." He grinned. "If I told how long ago, might bring back the eels. My own fault: door open and drunker than seven thousand dollars. I told him to send off his friends, and I'd take that damn ice punch—I don't remember. I really didn't care. Didn't care a damn. And that pleased him somehow. Hasn't bothered me—for money—since."

"He was alone last night. And he took a check. But it was unsigned."

"Alone? Didn't make you sign?" Tanner looked away. DeFord said nothing. "Forget it, neighbor. See any whiskey in my face? . . . Thought not. Took me two days to dry it out." His weathered handsome face turned down to watch his umbrella beat its purposeless tattoo, but his eyes crept up toward DeFord. "I'm scared to the core of these pair of sieves I call a liver. Who the hell's going to hire an old—"

"That isn't so."

"Thanks. Shock of the morning, I guess. And that damn cold shower. Hate those things. You take cold showers, DeFord? . . . Didn't think so."

"Mr. Tanner," DeFord said, thinking: Well why not? You have to start somewhere. "Perhaps you could advise me—"

"About Raven?" Tanner's face jumped. "Out of the question. You see, I already—represent Mr.—Joseph—Raven . . ."

"I see." Well, he thought, make it easy on yourself, mister.

"Wait." Tanner's right hand combed his long yellow-white hair. "Let's talk about this later. You see, Raven . . . that is"—he drew himself up—"I need—how shall I say"—he aimed his umbrella westward—"a fresh case. A piece of good work. A new day."

DeFord grunted. "Had something like that in mind for myself."

"Of course." Tanner studied him. "Should have sensed that. But then—when the underside of your bed shelters every creepy, crawly—plays all hell with your perceptions. So. We'll proceed then, this evening. Yes. You'll bring me luck, neighbor. Maybe we'll be lucky for each other, who knows. No whiskey in my face at all? It's the black Irish complexion. Ginsburg-Murphys the clan of us. Well, see you this evening." Umbrella jammed under his arm, Tanner marched off, gleaming shoes squeaking the silent street.

The white dog chose to walk with DeFord. "Tired of going it alone? You want to throw in on this chore too? If you want a man, you'll have to put up with a name.

Here, Sheriff!" But the dog squatted just beyond reach and smiled with his teeth.

At Elizabeth and Prince a derelict in a tattered coat stopped them, pointed, and beyond his blackened forefinger DeFord saw a bill at the grating across the street. The derelict wet his lips, face cramped with helplessness and rage.

DeFord grunted, crossed over to the grating, folded the bill and returned. "Yours? Did you lose it?" He shoved the bill into the man's pocket. "Best take better care of your money."

◇ ◇ ◇

Dee Bee sinks weakly onto the curb of his block and watches old lumberjack with the dirty white dog move down Elizabeth Street. His eyes are glazed, his senses exhausted; only his fingers move, stroking the crisp bulge in his breast pocket. "Memo," he whispers. "Memo . . ." But nothing comes.

Careful! Danger! A pair of pointed shoes, one black, the other the color of rancid butter, slide up to him and stop. Dee Bee is rigid with fright. Easy. Easy. "Hello, Proudhomme."

The bleached mannequin's face bends down. "Friend of yours, Dee Bee? Don't shake your head, darling. He gave you something. I saw."

"My silk—it blew over the curb." Dee Bee fumbles and produces a square of dirty pink silk.

"Where's he going, darling? Where's he headed?" Proudhomme's clothes smell damp, wormy, and the silk trembles in Dee Bee's hand. "Never mind, you filthy old bitch. I'll find out myself."

When the shoes mince away, Dee Bee smooths his silk carefully, tucks it into a pocket and scuttles to his doorway, where he slowly unfolds the bill. He stares. It is a fiver.

II

Stunned by the sun, the Bowery lies quiet at its limbo hour: six A.M. To its south in the financial area, a few vans disgorge the tons of paper soon to be filled with speculations, hints, suggestions, advice, demands, threats, entreaties, promises; it is completely deserted farther north, where a block of diamond markets, windows framed in cold blue silver, lies caged and mined with hidden wires and triggered alarms; gem slivers on black velvet, like stars at the bottom of a well, await the wrists, fingers, necks, ears of those with the paper promises. Farther north, where elevated trains once kept the street in shadow, it is now open to the sun like a wound blotched with pawnshops, flophouses, bloodybuckets, wineshops, greasy spoons, barber colleges, missions, all interlaced with plumbing stores—this part haunted at every hour by disheveled men who pass gleaming windows of faucets, pipes, sinks, showers and toilets like invertebrates drifting through some sunken Atlantis. Finally to its very north the Bowery is again silent, where the city's most venerable college blocks its way with three-hundred-year-old wrought iron and brick. From money through despair to knowledge, and only the place of despair is never deserted.

On a narrow concrete island in the middle of Bowery, DeFord stood marooned, waiting for Sheriff to finish placing his sign on the wheels of a milk truck. He was thinking: Why must I ignore this place or find myself believing it's the center of the world? Naked. Naked. Great misfortune, great ugliness, great failure—people have no reverence for it. Who said that . . . ? A very old man he had met in the park. A Mr. Codgers. Yes. Sheriff squeezed the last drop to the truck's right rear. "We'll cross now," DeFord said, and walked east on Delancey, looking for help-wanted signs . . . Naked.

Twelve empty electric chairs waited in a beauty salon, choked drugstore windows advertised kosher vitamins, and a corner truss shop displayed seven windows of flesh-colored supports, huge studded harnesses, the jocks of heroes. At Essex a Brooklyn subway shook the concrete beneath him as he walked toward a very small park crowded with saplings that reached out from holes bored in the concrete. There he paused, watching two old men crouched motionless over a cement chess table. One of them was slowly reaching for his knight when a truck swung around the corner, and under its wheels DeFord heard a backbone-snap sever the scream of a dog.

"Sheriff!"

His white mongrel still sat beside him, but a black-and-tan dragged its broken hindquarters toward the curb. The trucker climbed down heavily and bent over the hound. "I hope no kid owned this," he said, and looked up at DeFord as if for a release. He stood arms akimbo, heavy-gutted, nodding his head at nothing. "Hope it wasn't—"

"Don't touch him!" A policeman stepped from a patrol car behind the truck. "They'll bite when they're hit." The trucker turned aside when the policeman pushed at the black-and-tan with his night stick. "No collar—belongs to nobody." The stick flashed, cracked hard between the wild eyes, and the dog went limp. Then the stick pointed at Sheriff. "That your mutt, pops? Get a license for him, or I'll have to take him in."

As the patrol car pulled away, the trucker spat and said to no one in particular, "Shit and you makes nothing." Then he hauled himself into his cab, mashed gears and drove on.

The two old men crouched over the cement table had not looked up from their game.

Naked. Naked, thought DeFord. "Let's get some breakfast, Sheriff." They walked past the sanitation department under the Williamsburg Bridge approach, and as he came out into the sun he thought suddenly: Perhaps it is not that it is too naked for me, but that nothing else is naked enough to match it.

At a stationery store just opening near East River Park, DeFord spent his last money for stale cupcakes to share with Sheriff in the park. It would not be easy to get a stake; he realized with a blurred feeling that he had been through it all many times before. But I was different then. How many men have I been? I accept each of them, each is me, yet I could never bring them all together. No. They would all want pancakes first thing in the morning and take coffee black but argue everything else. One other thing was true now: they would all have a bad heart.

Ahead the East River rippled north and south, and almost above, the Williamsburg Bridge made miniatures of the barges slipping through the dark water. Everything entering its shadow became a toy over which the bridge was a huge warped plank, suspended from Manhattan to Brooklyn by wrist-thin wires. Above the river rolling at its stanchions, gulls rose and fell in the skein of cables; clouds corrugated with blue dragged beneath the sun, bringing dapples of shadow that depressed him. Enough of this, he thought, and went toward the river, coming into a path that led into the secret places under the great bridge.

Codgers, brush in hand, pants rolled above old man's ankles, thin body erect somewhere beneath a thick turtleneck sweater, peered over a wide canvas at the bridge, muttering, "Marchant, *Woman at the Opera,* fifty thousand francs, Paris, 1908; Gilespie, *Untitled,* twenty-eight thousand francs, Vienna, 1911." DeFord came from behind and coughed. In his high old man's voice Codgers said, "Proudhomme, I have eighty-five cents in my watch pocket, but you'll have to kill me for it."

"Mr. Codgers?"

"Ah, Mr. DeFord." His voice seemed to come from a small brittle bone under his sweater. "I thought you were Proudhomme come to beg. Saw him sneaking around a moment ago."

"Don't let me disturb your work."

"I won't." Codgers swiveled and touched just enough gray to the shadowy pockets of his bridge to suggest something prehistoric about it. "The light is interesting this morning. Constantly caught in that thing." He daubed a stanchion edge bright ivory, then thoughtfully cleaned his brushes and laid his hands like folded parchment over his lap. "Let's see, it's been a week since we've talked. So you've been to the clinic again. I trust you are mending well?"

"Yes." Damn, he thought, I've an appointment this

afternoon. I musn't forget. Must not stop now. Gather up. Keep on with everything. "Will you paint a boat in, or just the bridge?"

"Bridge? A word, Mr. DeFord. There are words for everything: bridge, tree, sea gull, love. But once there weren't words. The experience of this bridge was new, wordless—something that at this hour in this light exploded with possibility, the consequence beyond the imagination of its creator. That was when we were children. So I want to put back into what you call a bridge what we saw when we were children."

"The mystery."

"No. Once I wanted that, but I tired quickly of mystery. I want to put back into it the adventure of it." Codgers tucked his high black shoes under his stool. "If I keep with it too long this morning, I'll find myself lying, painting adventure I no longer feel. Of course, when I lie, I lie out of love. Love becomes lie, becomes art. And so good proceeds from evil." His polished face crinkled. "You do not believe in evil, do you? You must, Mr. DeFord, you must."

DeFord was silent. What do I know of this man? Nothing. Yet you have to start somewhere.

Sheriff moved to sniff Codger's paintbox, and the old man squeaked over his shoulder, "Your dog is hungry."

"I haven't been able to feed him properly. Last night Joe Raven stole my pension check."

"Raven, Mr. DeFord? When had you met him before last night? . . . Never, you say? No. No. He had met you, then. You had offended him. Yes. Perhaps you carry your head too high, you whistle, you smile." Codgers turned to face him. "But this is not the help you seek."

"I want my check back, and I'll be needing a stakeover till the next."

Motionless, face stiff as a varnished puppet's, Codgers

held his ancient child's hands smooth and upturned on his lap, their white palms open as if to receive the questions his lips kept back. Staring at him, DeFord felt a slow ebbing of energy, and under his ribs an aching hollowness drained his groin, leaving an empty place where his tired heart reverberated. I must collect myself. Somehow I must get through this week and out of here. His limbs felt useless and heavy. My God, what has happened to me? What will become of me? Why me? Why has this happened to me? Why not—? But he could think of no one else, and with an effort that seemed impossible he pulled himself erect on the hard bench. I will get through this nightmare. I will go home at last. I shall not lose.

Codgers stirred, blinked, shrugged. "Of course, that explains Proudhomme—he's following to see if you go to the police. And you haven't . . . I didn't think so. But he still follows. Therefore Raven is not finished. I would guess the check is unsigned . . . Then you may have a chance of retrieving your check. Only if Raven does not suspect you care that much for it. Your inclination is to disagree, I'm sure. Do I know the man? you want to ask. Yes, I know Raven. Do you?"

Only the ice pick— "Ahhh," DeFord whispered, the memory sinking to his heart. He did say he'd kill me. "I remember now. But not his face . . ."

"It is a mask. Once I asked if I could paint him. He would not answer me." Codgers peered at him, then turned to his canvas, and his eyes opened perfectly round as he absently mixed black and green oils with a wispy brush. "The next day he fell from that bridge. I saw it. Unfortunately it did not kill him. But it made him . . ." While he spoke he worked a hint of mold into the shadows on his canvas. "There is something lizardlike about those hidden, always sunless places, is there not? Must be bats, the smell of fungus." He looked back at DeFord. "So he threatened you?" he asked carefully. "How do I know? Because Raven would have obliged you to sign your check or not have bothered himself with it—unless in you he has found someone . . . no matter. However, if I am right he would start with threats."

DeFord stiffened. This is not sense, this is—

"A high-iron man," squeaked Codgers. "He was a high-iron man. He worked on a beam the width of a shovel. He fell, leaning far out into a wind, trying to tempt a fish hawk with a bit of ham sandwich. They say he was laughing. Then suddenly there was no wind—as if someone had turned a switch, dropped a hand or for an instant stopped caring. And down he went."

DeFord stood. "I will find him and talk with him."

Codgers turned petulantly to his canvas. "He has already found you. And you could not talk to him." He pointed his brush at the stanchion of his bridge. "Johnie Leggatt lives out there. He could talk to Raven. Although he might not be able to retrieve your check, he could find out about—the threat. Perhaps he could get you a job. He knows everyone."

"He lives on the river?"

"There is a fishline along the ladder from the bridge deck to the first stanchion. You will have to lower a note. He should come up sober, he may come drunk, but I hope he has enough sense left not to try it hung over."

"Thanks the same. It's not my way."

"You insult me, assuming I have energies for games, Mr. DeFord. Especially with strangers." His faded eyes burned. "I advise you to enlist Johnie's help because I feel responsible for your situation. You see—it is me Raven wants to kill. Me. Perhaps he knows this, perhaps not. Still, he cannot kill me—I no longer care. And that he does know . . . When you tell Leggatt I have sent you, he will come up. He owes me that."

"Drunk?"

"You certainly do pry with your stubbornness." Codgers' head quivered on the wrinkled stalk of his neck. "If Leggatt is drunk he owes me no favor. For my advice was that he should live on the river. If it was effective he may be sober or hung over, but at this time of day he should not be drunk. He should be working. And if so, he will be quite aware of the obligation."

DeFord whistled Sheriff and stood looking out at the river, numbed and angry. I need no one.

Codgers was absorbed again in his canvas, hand folded, legs tucked under. "A man named Devornet sold a painting in Paris in 1911 for thirty thousand francs. Then, Mr. DeFord, a franc was a franc. Have you ever heard of him? . . . Neither has anyone else, but he did sell it. Now it is not only worthless but lost . . . You have decided you do not need Leggatt, or anyone. I would disagree. I offer a story they tell on the Bowery. That once Joe Raven lost four fingers in a broken-bottle fight and regrew them in a month. Of course you will not choose to believe that, Mr. DeFord. But I, on the contrary, I believe everything."

◇ ◇ ◇

On the pedestrian walk Sheriff sat grinning, while DeFord peered over the railing at the ladder plunging toward the river below and the stanchion floating like a waterlogged cork. He played out the remaining coils of Leggatt's fishline, saw his note flash white as a wind caught it and the line bellied but sank again. Using his father's IWW card as a sinker, he watched it twirl two hundred feet below, carrying his note out of sight. A figure stepped from the shadows, waved; the line jerked and struggled. DeFord closed his eyes, turned his face to the sun, and his dizziness lifted. When the line went tight, then limp three slow times, he leaned away from the edge and wound it from palm to crooked elbow. He reread his own note: "Raven has threatened me. Mr. Codgers said you could help. DeFord." Beneath it Leggatt had scrawled: "Ah, DeFord! Ah, humanity! Ah, idiocy!" The weighted IWW card was gone; in its place three crushed empty paint tubes.

He felt suddenly strong, invigorated, confident. Yes, I am being a fool, he thought, crouching and offering his hand to Sheriff. "You have more sense than all of us." Leaning over the railing, he watched Leggatt mount the ladder: a darkened miniature, face blinking white. Yet as Leggatt crept larger, DeFord's dizziness returned. What if he loses strength and I have to climb after him? I would do it. I would have to do it. The thought of starting down the ladder was so terrible he closed his eyes and counted his heart until the vertigo passed. When he opened them Leggatt rested halfway, like a windblown scarecrow. His body was muscled, and his work shirt and denim appeared to have been donned wet, then dried as an afterthought. DeFord watched him wrap one leg in the rungs and adjust his bundle carelessly, the wind riffling his cuffs and moaning the cables above. He climbed irregularly—at times negligently, then a burst of climbing, then lean back to smile upwards. At the end of each burst Leggatt's face lifted, until DeFord thought he recognized something familiar. Watching the strain of the climb knot Leggatt's shoulders and neck, DeFord thought he was seeing himself, forty-eight years ago in Michigan. No. It is this naked part of the city. And Raven. And the hospital. No, it is hardly the same face.

As Leggatt ascended, DeFord realized there was nothing, absolutely nothing, of habit in the man at all.

III

Bent like a hinge under his roll of canvases and frames, Leggatt stared at the city, while DeFord's memory slipped back to a peddler draped over a fence line, tossing wild grape seeds into freshly turned hedge furrows. That had been—outside Seattle perhaps. The peddler had seeded likely places all the way from Delaware. "To see where I've been, ever I care to come back again."

Leggatt worked the cramps from his fingers and straightened: a young face, scarless, with a remote smile at the corners of the mouth, yet pinched at the eyes as if from thirty-odd years of madness, ambition or both. His brittle irises had just enough gray to soften if they rested long enough on one thing, but he kept them busy plucking at various objects, as if seeking the keylog in a jam. "There's hands for you. Coal-black and just as steady." He studied his palms with respect.

DeFord felt uncomfortably hesitant and shy. "I'm sorry you had to come up for me," he wanted to say, but he said nothing, so Leggatt flung his arms over the railing and whistled through his teeth while his eyes ranged the city and his stiff sooty hands lay against the sky. Yes, they are real hands now, DeFord thought, and the buildings are buildings.

When Leggatt fished in his breast pocket, Sheriff's eyes riveted, then slumped, losing interest, when a bent cigarette emerged. "Is he always that hungry, or did Raven take everything you had?"

"All but some silver. But I hadn't signed the check."

Leggatt was staring as if he wanted to turn DeFord's face gently into the sun to read something there, and DeFord found himself wiping his jaw with the flat of his hand, thinking the instant he gestured: I have nothing to fear. Yet Leggatt seemed to find what he expected, for he smiled and looked away. "I know a place to wash up. Then we'll get started."

They walked where the bridge arched over the park and flooded Delancey Street with cars, Sheriff trotting between them; Leggatt swung ahead with the careless ease DeFord had begun to notice in younger men since his heart had faltered. It never irritated him before; actually, nothing other people did or chose not to do had troubled him for years. It was still a big country where he had built the last of other people's houses, bigger country where he had finally built his own. If you stop to figure it, he thought, trying to pass over his annoyance with—what? Leggatt's neck? Yes, the way it appeared stiff and set—anyway, if you figured it, this was big country, and he damn well knew his part of it enough to keep out of everyone's way. Leggatt's neck did annoy him; it was exactly his own: short for his height, so that his ears seemed long and his shoulders slow to move. Every morning it's probably just stiff enough he has to take his head in his hands and twist it loose. One day when he's sixty or so, he'll be wondering what he's forgotten until he realizes his neck isn't stiff any more. Then for a long time he'll miss the pain of putting himself straight first thing in the day. Simply identifying with that insignificant a part of Leggatt's future made DeFord uncomfortable. I know something he does not, but it would be no good to tell him, even if I wanted to.

Over the park, the shrubs below boxed in concrete, Leggatt jerked his chin toward a row of benches surrounding a playground. Proudhomme, legs crossed tightly at his crotch, butter shoe glinting in the sun, sat on a bench near the playground's leaky fountain. His arms were wide and his woman's shirt open to his belt, white flesh the color of an exposed root, his body sprawled so that any thirsty child had to press by to drink. "Unzip and let the sun shine in!" Leggatt yelled down. "Maybe it will grow."

Proudhomme spread his thighs, passed two fingers over his crotch and blew a kiss upwards.

"Faggots, pimps, fairies, fops, giggling lisping perverts." Leggatt grinned. "How sterile. That's why they parade so, DeFord—to camouflage the nothing where their guts should be. Was he with Raven last night?"

DeFord shook his head, interested yet annoyed with Leggatt's extravagance. "Raven was alone, Mr. Leggatt. He had an ice pick, and I was certain he would use it. If I hadn't recently been in a hospital I'd have—"

"Thrown him into the street." Leggatt's face softened. "I haven't thought anything else since I read your note. But Proudhomme and a thing named Crook help Joe drink his insurance check each week. So I assume they're running together. Anyway, Proudhomme's not important."

They walked parallel to the traffic following the concrete mesh east to the narrow river levee. The bench where Proudhomme had lurked was empty, but children's wet tracks carefully circled where the fountain spilled over gravel and cigarette butts like some tepid waterhole. As they passed the playground, one of the smaller children tripped and took his fall on the palms of his hands. DeFord stopped and watched the child drift in circles, massaging red palms on baggy trousers as if to rub off the pain. The game—one child chosen by the eldest, then run by the pack until cornered and his hat snatched—continued without the casualty, who sat studying his fellows through bouts of tears, hands held respectfully from his sides. DeFord found himself listening for his heart, and remembering the fury of his attack, he felt a sudden vicious contraction twisting into him for such an impossibly extended moment it seemed not so much intended to kill, but rather an unimaginable punishment for some half nerveless creature a hundred times his size. He shuddered at the lesson and walked closer to Leggatt.

"Ah. Here's where Joe spent the morning." On the pavement a chalk circle had been divided into seven sections, and four were crowded with elaborate stick figures. "How much cash did he take?"

"Just shy of seven dollars."

"Well, he had twenty cents this morning and was trying to find someone to buddy in another fifteen to fill out a pint."

"Because he'd sent Proudhomme to follow me. But what about his other friend?"

"Crook? He was, or is, sleeping off his share of your six and change. Too bad you hadn't more to lose." He bent over Raven's drawing. "Funny thing, they'll get better the drunker he is."

"I should have more money for Raven to steal?" De-

Ford snapped. Yet he found himself forcing a smile over his anger when Leggatt turned.

"Not for Joe to steal, Mr. DeFord. For Crook to tie onto a three-day blow." They stared at each other, Sheriff between them on Raven's circle, DeFord stiffening as the brittleness came into Leggatt's eyes. "You know, Mr. DeFord, I climbed that bridge for Codgers, but when I go back down, it won't be for Codgers or anyone else. I sleep just over the water—about the same as having a loaded pistol under your pillow if you're the type to think of slipping in—anyway, it's a great consolation. After a night's rest I swim, catch a flounder or two and fry a decent meal. I have a hot plate, paints, even electricity—lights to warn the tugboats off. So nothing grows on me out there but what I cart down on my back."

There had been a time, DeFord thought, when I could stand here and listen to this, then whistle my dog and go down the road. "There was a time," he wanted to say. His eyes dropped where Sheriff sat without expression, then turned stubbornly up at Leggatt to wait him out.

"If you want a job, I may be able to help."

"I'd appreciate that."

"Sometime today I'm supposed to stop at my brother's gallery, but I won't. However, I will take these canvases to the old monkey's—Codgers' loft. We can eat something there."

"I'd appreciate that too."

So they walked together, Leggatt whistling through his teeth and DeFord breathing the musky cool river in long drafts and thinking: I must seem a crotchety old man. Well, no matter. He is just as mulish, and I suppose his extravagance is the way of everything he does: "I'm supposed to . . . but I won't." I can get used to it soon enough; I'll just have to make room for it.

Ahead at a *boucha* court, old peasant men in berets and baggy unmatched suits were carefully rolling worn wooden balls. Watching their stubby hands caress and pitch in slow rolling arcs, DeFord felt better. "Why would you have this Crook so drunk?"

Leggatt said nothing until they came to a cement blockhouse squatting beneath a Grecian roof that seemed hurriedly mounted and, as afterthought, apologetically stained with tea. Under a porcelain MEN sign someone had crayoned: "The Bird Lives and Walks among You." "Because Crook does all Joe's bad work," Leggatt answered as he pushed open the door with his toe.

A beam of sunlight plunged from a clerestory window to a toilet bowl where a Negro sat, pants about his ankles, jacket cowled over his head. Around him a half dozen men were making their ablutions, painfully slow, in such a fog of sweat, Lysol and urine DeFord was momentarily stunned. The closing door dropped everything into shadow, but a cigarette glowed under the Negro's jacket as he sucked, held his breath, quivered, then sighed and nibbled the smoke trapped in his jacket. The latrine jerked alive when a man bawled, "Next!" and his hairy back wallowed up from a washbowl, wet shaved head buried under newspaper which thick hands massaged. "Who's got soap?" The soggy newsprint disintegrated, revealing a glistening head and a round glaring face. "Johnie! Is it working for you? Who's got some soap?"

"Hello, Remember." Leggatt passed his back roll to DeFord, extracted a towel and soap and peeled his shirt. "Yes, things are working."

"For crissake. I asked if anybody had soap!"

Leggatt lathered his hands. "You didn't ask me."

"So I left my manners up river. No—that isn't true—I never had none to leave. May I use your soap when you're finished?"

"Of course. Then let's talk. I want to ask you about a job."

"A what? Jesus, Johnie, that never works."

At the toilet a cigarette burned a hole in the cowl's shadow. "Ahh, ahh, ahhhh." A dark hand cupped eddies and drank them in. "Ahhh . . . I saw." The Negro let his jacket fall and eased up his trousers.

"It worked?"

"Yesss. I am the Man. I am Babe Jesus." He rocked off the seat and rose slowly, face flowering into the sun.

"If you're Jesus"—Remember pointed to a long ribbon of excrement—"what the hell's that?"

The Negro regarded his turd. "The Mystery, man. The Mystery."

Someone said, "This is a bad hole to blow that stuff. The uncles will get you."

"I am no handkerchief head, man. I am the Babe Jesus."

A bear with a bald head waddled through the sunlight and held his hand for Leggatt's soap. "That Babe's Mystery is the color of beefstock and beans."

The smell of marijuana clinging to him, the Babe swayed in his shaft of sunlight. "Mission people right, man. Christ is in me. Yesss."

Another in a corner said, "Fucking hophead Christian. Let's knock him in the fucking eyes and get him the fuck out a here. Only fucking place we got left to clean the fuck up."

"You're as winy beat over as any of us," said Remember. "And not that much blacker. How come you eat mission soup?"

" 'Cause I have seen, man. And I'm goin' to tell you all—"

"That fucking settles it! When they send their fucking finks into a man's fucking bathroom—"

"Easy." Leggatt came from the shadows, drying his arms. "Let's bring him down."

Someone said, "Either bring him down, Johnie, or we'll throw him out. He'll get us all busted."

Leggatt faced the Babe over the toilet and finished drying his arms. "Your man Jesus was interesting but not great. Your man Jesus was equivocal, unclear and short of temper."

"Ahh, ahh." The Babe found a smell of the weed on his fingers.

"There was too much of the priest in Jesus. He raged at His people because they could not understand Him. But if they couldn't, it was His fault. His creations turned out badly—"

"Noo, man."

"—so He threatened them. And when they could not understand, He took upon himself all their guilt so they would feel even guiltier."

"Nooo, man. Nooo."

"Admittedly he was quite patient at times and had a gentle understanding—especially with children. But there was too much Man in Him. He hinted at what would come after, then went His way satisfied."

"Ah, ahh, ahhh." Babe Jesus discovered a wisp on his lapel and undulated in the sun.

"Tell him!" exploded Remember over his brackish suds as he danced for the proffered towel.

"He made His people feel inadequate and sick because they would forever not be great. And He made them even guiltier because He took their guilt upon Himself. He knew all this, but the Man in Him said, 'It is enough to show them I know so future generations can wonder My wisdom and understanding.' Being a man, that was enough. But the God seeker in Him was bothered by His not *doing* anything about it. So do you know how He got around that?" Leggatt unrolled a jacket from his pack and slipped it on.

"Noo. Nooo, man." The swaying Babe frantically snuffed for the last of the weed. "You're bringing me down, man, you're bringing me down."

"He went away. That's what He did. He went away." Leggatt flushed the mystery down the bowl.

"Ahhh, man. You've brought me down."

"He was an interesting god but not a great one. But then again, a well-respected, nourishing god once a week, and what the hell."

Remember opened the door, and DeFord stepped ahead.

Urine, sweat, Lysol, burnt marijuana vanished.

◇ ◇ ◇

A moth-eaten bear of a man wrapped in disheveled fading tatters, humps of seldom used muscle lumpy under what once had been clothing, Remember Baker sat on his hands and spoke of shoe polish, floor wax, bay rum, perfume, antifreeze, denatured alcohol, gasoline, muskydoodle port and a few of the more effective combinations, distillations and variations: pink ladies, sneaky Petes, white elephants and smoke. "They all work," he said. He spoke of the rubbydubs, loners, jockers, punks, winos and lushes for whom they worked and the fleabags, blinkies, wingies, fruitcakes, feebs, stiffies and halfies who could not always make them work. Finally he spoke of money: one could Sunday-bootleg (you needed capital and protection or someone would put the hammer to you), one could steal for the thieves' market which materialized each morning in front of the Bowery Mission (Remember did not believe in stealing; it did not work for him), one could scrounge for deposit bottles or peddle trinkets uptown or just plain beg (which was all right).

Or sell your blood. "No," he corrected, "I am lying again. Bumming's no good. The best is selling blood. Seven, eight dollars a pint, but never less than five. The city always needs blood. If nothing else works, blood will."

"I want a job," said DeFord.

Remember looked at Leggatt. "Jesus, I thought he wanted money."

"That wasn't what I said."

"Yeah, Johnie, I'm lying again. I remember now."

DeFord stood and whistled to Sheriff. He had almost been angry again with Leggatt, but now he was angry with himself. It will do me no good to throw in with the man. "Doesn't make any difference. Thank you for your trouble anyway."

"No difference!" Remember said. "Why, it makes all the difference in the world! You got to know if you're lying. You can't forget, you know. You can't let yourself forget—then what's happened never happened like. See?"

"Hey," Leggatt soothed, "you got the best head job I've ever seen."

Remember grinned and lowered his shaved head. "Yeah, not even a nick. My buddy at the college does it free. He was up river too." His eyes closed and his hands pushed under his thighs. "He never got as far as me, though." He eased his thick hands into his lap and studied them.

DeFord said, "This is big country."

"Run into Joe Raven lately?" Leggatt asked quickly.

"For you maybe . . . no, Johnie," Remember said, "but Crook was climbing out under a table at the One Miler an hour ago. Even Bert was afraid to get close. You looking for him?"

"I think he'll be looking for us."

"I don't want to hear about it. Don't want to know anything about it— Hey, you heading for the block? Buy you a drink. You sure gave that hophead a run, Johnie. You were real good in there."

DeFord waited, thinking: I should try on my own. I don't need anyone. But he waited, nonetheless.

"No, thanks, Remember, maybe some other time."

Remember rocked on his hands. "Yeah, it's dry work. But I don't forget. That's the thing."

◇ ◇ ◇

In three weeks in the city DeFord's sense of smell narrowed to a bland, oppressive odor—part asphalt, part fresh produce, part clothing, pomades, perfume, leather, and the deodorants covering the people beneath it all, who had their particular odors as well. This suspension wafted with a vapor of street exhaust which DeFord imagined hung above the concrete in thinning layers. His sight, however, had adjusted with greater reluctance to the flashy clothing boiling up and down the sidewalks, the car caravans leaping to each green light, and the serrated lines of crowded buildings. Yet his ears could not adjust, and the city remained a cacophony of jangled cries.

They passed an Italian, a Jewish, a Spanish block, and came to the narrow park between Chrystie and Forsyth, where Leggatt indicated a bench. DeFord took one of his pills and swallowed it dry as his confusion ebbed.

"I can never do that—always sticks in my throat." Leggatt's eyes crinkled. "You can get used to anything, I suppose."

"All my life I've shaved with a straight razor from a pan of water. No soap. That's habit too."

Leggatt had plucked DeFord's tin-framed IWW card from his pocket and was scraping it over his cheek. "I could as well with this. You've kept it in very good condition, but it seems—faded. Anyway, I was afraid you might lose it when you retrieved the line. Shall I get us some breakfast?"

"Not faded—waterlogged. No, thank you, I'll let breakfast wait."

"You'll need some money to eat on." Leggatt tapped the stained card. "I can get a loan on this, you know. There's a fellow nearby who collects them. Maybe give me three, four dollars." Without waiting for an answer, he started across the street, then turned and skipped back up on the curb. "Would you do something for me? I can't print worth a damn. Would you copy the three messages here onto separate sheets? They shouldn't be in my handwriting anyway." Leggatt drew pencil and papers from his pocket, and again without waiting for an answer, loped across the street. DeFord grunted and worked quickly so he would not have to think about the lie of the pawned card.

> This is a warning. Stop this distribution of your insidious immoral communistic oil tracts. We have watched the development of your atheistic un-American socialist trends and—

He copied, then stopped. What in God's name—? First he lies about pawning a worthless souvenir so I won't feel in his debt; then he involves me in this nonsense. Well, it's his business. DeFord finished the first and second cards, working slowly now to stretch the time. But when the third was done he was still alone, so he turned his face to the sun and shut his eyes.

◇ ◇ ◇

It was shortly after his father died. For the first time in years his mind caught at the image of his father erect in a Michigan-boardinghouse bed, slowly drowning of pneumonia, and the doubt always accompanying the memory:

should he have stayed in Michigan? No, he had been right! Just as right a year later in Colorado. Forty-seven years ago America was even bigger country than he had expected, and if he had to walk with his *Carpenter's Manual* to the very end of it, he would. He did not want to live where men were tossed into scaler ponds or shot down clinging to their own pole fences.

Not because a DeFord always seemed to lose no matter who won: what the DeFords lost did not really matter to him, only the insult of losing, only the senselessness of losing, the wretchedness, the littleness of losing. That was why he hated the Bowery—not the failure it contained, he could forgive men that, but the shame of it. It was unnecessary. This was still America, and if in America there was only one thing possible, if only one thing had ever been possible, it was that a man could someday finally settle on his own and stay out of everyone else's way. That he now believed without question, as he had believed in Michigan, as he had been determined in Colorado a year later, as it had kept him walking thirty-five miles of steel track in blinding sun, as it had prodded him, goaded him, promised and wrenched him up and down the Far West until he had been able to prove it. His determination to prove his country was big enough for him and so for everyone, for anyone, had been his woman, his family, his religion since—when? Since Colorado, if such a thing begins any one place.

When he was younger he had sometimes spoken of his faith that there were forgotten places, secret places in his great country where a man might live alone. So there had been accusers. "You'll never find such a place, Lyle," his father had said. "It's never existed. It's always been a dream, always a delusion. Everything worth space has been done by people who knew that. This country is this room and the mill, it's that red card in my pocket and those poor devils who tossed me into the scaler pond. There won't be anything different, no matter where you go." Four days later DeFord walked from his father's grave through a line of loggers who muttered apologies, excuses, and condolences. That night he discovered the red card was as good as a ticket for a whole series of freight trains. But he ran out of food money at a siding in Craig, a small Colorado town which still retained wooden sidewalks, false store fronts, and an old sheriff who once had to shoot back at an armed drunk and misjudged, killing the man. So the town had the makings of its legend, and no matter how thoroughly the remorseful sheriff talked it down, when he died, it would remain as myth. Craig had waited long enough for its Western tradition and felt as deserving as any town.

The Great War had not touched Craig as directly as the lumber mills of Michigan, but it very favorably affected sugar beet prices, which stimulated the farmers to mortgage heavily and sink many deep wells to irrigate the dry-land wheat acreage. The creeping ditches changed everything: fifteen-acre wheatland yielded ninety to a hundred bushels; sugar beets bulged like swollen teeth under their coarse mattock of green leaf; the farmers irrigated at night to cut evaporation, and during the darkest hours, under a prairie sky shattered with stars, they gathered at the field corners to gossip, knots of carbide lamps flickering like the pickets of some vast battleground. During the day an army of underpaid Mexican laborers hoed the tuberous beets. But it was expensive farming; the new crop demanded close cooperation, and the Water Board, the Beet Board, the Ditch Board, at first innocently contrived, commanded more and more power, made more and more decisions, entangling the entire valley in a skein of interlocking water rights, railroad spurs, and public investment. That is, they entangled everyone but a man named Anderson, who had come down from Utah with his wife and daughter, and with great luck and innocence, bought a place just before the water boom. He kept his three hundred acres along the valley's main drainage in alfalfa for his feeder stock and horses.

Anderson did not object that the town called him a one-wife Mormon and former lieutenant to the Salt Lake City war councillor himself. He had lost three sons in the Mormon wars, and after all, Craig was wanting on local melodrama. Anderson did not object when at the same time that the town was politely asking permission to cut an emergency ditch through his right of way to his stream frontage, the picket gossip damned him as a Mexican lover. He reasoned that his neighbors had a right to some of his water, and if they paid their help a third of what he paid his, after all, prosperity had come late, so perhaps they could not be expected to know that nothing is built with slave labor guiltlessly. He said nothing when the town allowed its Klan to keep the Mexicans in order; he did nothing when they began to draw steadily on the emergency ditch; he even ignored field gossip that his daughter was really a second wife. He was a latecomer; he was a refugee; he had lost family, religion, and home; and again, Craig was lean on any formal history or tradition with which such things could be compared. But in an especially dry summer when their ditch threatened to drain his stock water, he told them to trim their waterheads. When they did not, he filed immediate suit against the town Water Board, and the county had to support him.

Anderson could accept anything but that his stock should want for the sake of thirsty beets.

DeFord slipped from a freight car just at the time Anderson needed a new sluice gate, and stayed on to repair it periodically when it was attacked at night with crowbars. Actually, things went quite well for half a year, while DeFord kept himself in room and board building and repairing fence lines. His feeling of rootlessness and despair gradually ebbed. Anderson seemed to like him, and if there had been time, probably would have moved him—IWW card, *Carpenter's Manual,* and all—into his house and sat him at his table. The daughter, referred to in the fields at night as Anderson's sleeping wife, was self-contained, quiet, and handsome. She and DeFord were cautiously getting to know each other when one morning Anderson went out early to check his head gate and someone at quite close range fired two 12-gauge loads of buckshot into his chest. He was dead when DeFord reached him.

A group of neighbors coming from their beets with cold lamps in their hands ran over and stood like dumb cattle at the fence. DeFord remembered their shocked faces, numbed bodies rooted with backs to their fields as if to hide them from his accusing eyes. The aging sheriff could do nothing, but the town to a man came to the grave, and within a week a farmer close by moved quietly away, his farm purchased by the town, his crop viciously abandoned, as if the beets and the land itself had been responsible and their shame could be leached by the merciless sun. Instead of myth and hero, Craig had come into its guilt.

Even now, a lifetime later, DeFord knew he had been in love with the girl, but that the love had become confused with his helplessness, rage, and disgust. The neighbors called on the girl and her mother; men appeared to oversee the Mexican hands and pick the best as foreman; the town honored the water, sent gifts, waved hello, and tipped hats. The town forgave.

DeFord? He could not stomach it, so he left. Even though the girl said she would not come to him, that it was he who would have to return, he did not believe her. He said he would send for her when he had money; he walked out to the tracks and swung up on the first freight going west. Ten miles down the track, a brakeman dressed like a hobo but carrying a piece of heavy rubber hose refused to acknowledge the red card. "Off, bo." They faced each other in an empty cattle car.

"It's thirty-odd miles to the next town," DeFord reasoned.

"And ten miles back to Craig, wob." The brakeman shifted his hose and jerked a short-barreled Colt from a leather pouch sewed over his watch pocket. "Over the side, wob."

It took a long time for the train to dissolve on the tracks that narrowed to a sliver aimed at the horizon of Colorado drylands. By the time it was out of sight, DeFord had decided not to go back to Craig. If he had money the girl would have come with him, he thought. But even if it were his fault, the walk would be punishment enough, and when he found a place where people would leave him and his own to themselves it would atone for it all, wouldn't it?

Six or seven heavy black birds swung high over the tracks every few hours to check his progress, and that night dozens of snakes sought the warmth of the railbed. He promised himself two things: to always keep enough money on hand and to find a hidden place somewhere.

The money was not difficult—he was an excellent carpenter—but in the end it did not matter. The girl did not come when he sent for her.

◇ ◇ ◇

So what had been an excuse, a punishment, an atonement or perhaps simply a promise—had become a habit, a habit his heart and Joe Raven had finally broken.

"Well," he said aloud on the bench. "Well, I have my place, anyway. I have my place." Sheriff looked up, cocked his mouth, and when DeFord held out his hand the dog deigned to have his head scratched. "Guess I'll have to take you along when they let me leave, won't I?"

"I've invested some of your loan. Hope you don't mind." Leggatt pocketed his notes without a word, sat beside him and extracted sandwich makings from a paper bag. "There's a quarter pound of ground beef next to the milk. Perhaps you should feed the dog yourself . . . Like hot peppers?"

"If they're hot enough." DeFord unwrapped a brown handful of beef and laid it between his work boots. Sheriff squatted three feet away, his throat swallowing at nothing, eyes hard and narrowed.

"If he's demonstrating his manners, he's somewhat out of place." Leggatt held out a sandwich bag of small green peppers. "They bite."

DeFord plucked off a tiny fuse of a stem and tossed one into his mouth. Chewing steadily, he moved the hamburger from between his boots, and Sheriff bolted the meat in three bites, then squatted and fastened his eyes to the paper bag. "No manners there. He's boot shy."

"That certainly isn't out of place." Leggatt accepted a pepper and looked at it carefully. "They should be quite hot."

DeFord, working on his second pepper, tongue consumed with heat, said, "Is that right?"

Leggatt chewed and blinked while DeFord divided a sandwich and placed it out of boot range. Sheriff retrieved and swallowed twice. "Have another of those little things." DeFord offered a second and chewed his third, his nose swelling with heat and his tongue quivering. He spoke carefully: "There was a time now, when you could get yourself a real pepper."

Leggatt sucked air as if to yawn. "I know what you mean." His jaw moved jerkily.

DeFord calmly selected a big one and sucked. "There's two more."

But Leggatt took a long swallow of milk, closed his eyes and sighed. "Thanks, but I think I'll have a sandwich now."

They walked north to Houston, where the Bowery men with anything pawnable were easing toward the Market, those without poking trash cans and edging close to open shop stalls, all senses violently alert for any sign, any possible chance to pluck something, or cover for a friend who would, or see a dropped coin, a forgotten piece of fruit, an unguarded thing of any species—all of them, haves and have-nots, trying to filch the price of a pint before market opened.

"Ah." At the corner lay another chalk circle, six of seven sections with stick figures. Leggatt slipped his hands into his back pockets, cocked his head and stared down. "Your friend certainly is getting around this morning. He must have filled out on this corner."

"Then he'd be drinking somewhere."

"With the wino who helped him make it hanging around for his nickel's worth. It would seem they're not after you, wouldn't it?"

"It would seem that way."

"Fine, then. Just fine. We'll cross Bowery and go south; there are more stores open now. Then we'll come back north on the other side, and I'll see if anything's going in the buckets. Proudhomme's probably following you just long enough to see you didn't go to the police."

"You seem quite relieved."

Leggatt shrugged, grinned, then pulled his notes from his pocket. "No, best not," he muttered, then examining them, said, "Hell, might as well," and dealt them onto

Raven's circle. "You've a fine legible hand, DeFord. Thanks." He began to read aloud:

> "This is a warning. Stop this distribution of your insidious immoral communistic oil tracts. We have watched the development of your atheistic un-American socialist trends and demand a new exhibition.
>
> "Time runs low. Do not think that the tendency to Trotskyite internationalism in your last two oils will placate us. Remember what happened to Pollock and Camus.
>
> "Our people in Washington and abroad now have a full dossier on your anti-American Asiatic religiosity. Only public recanting can save you now."

"Not so bad after all." Using his knuckles, he stone-rubbed a Raven stick figure as signature to each note. Then he straightened, put a finger to his lips and said, "Not a word, DeFord." They began to walk. But farther along Houston, he put his hand on DeFord's shoulder. "Those were the hottest goddamn peppers I've ever eaten."

"Really?"

They stepped together into the sun and crossed Bowery, DeFord whistling to himself and feeling the warmth on his face. It was going to be a fine day. A fine, fine day after all.

◇ ◇ ◇

Ten o'clock. Dee Bee Smith has eaten his plate of fifteen-cent franks and beans served by a bartender with wine-stained underarms. A good man, Dee Bee thinks, half remembering when he snubbed all winos. He was a lush then: an aristocrat. Actually, he feels better as a wino—there's more truth to it—a lush always deceives himself. Dee Bee equates his becoming part of the sticky ways of muskydoodle with the final way of seeing things. Thereto-

fore he had deceived himself, but with his decision for wine the block was revealed. He knows They are waiting for him. He knows. He has made many mistakes, he admits to himself with great cunning, but the wine has been lucky for him and now he has his way. So long as he eats once each day and stays on his block, he is safe.

Digesting his beans, he leans against a wall and looks from end to end of his block for comfort. But something is wrong. His dirt-incrusted fingers twist his coat, and his lips move. Careful! He has been talking to himself! He claps the back of his hand over his lips, lowers his head and peers left and right. No, no one has heard. And he wasn't talking about it, anyway. It remains in his pocket; he can feel the crispness next to his silk. Dee Bee fingers the silk and smiles. Another thing They would take from him.

He moons along, pretending to watch the mission across the street, where a score of men lounge with old books, clothing, watches, razors, pieces of fruit, eyeglasses, shoes and paper bags. Some walk up and down past four or five men who stand visiting and smoking. Every so often a smoking man gestures and a man with something in his hands walks over, the smoker passes a coin, pockets the article and returns to smoking and visiting. The derelict hurries his coin to a bucket, or if it has been a good sale he shuffles to a wineshop. Dee Bee is pretending an interest, but actually he is counting the well-dressed people who pass. More and more of Them lately. Block is changing. Was it last night someone said They would soon clean up Bowery? He cannot remember; all his nights are confused.

"Hello, Dee Bee."

Ahhh! Dee Bee turns slowly, face a mask. It is only Johnie, but with him the man from earlier, the old lumberjack who brought the— Dee Bee pretends to wipe the corner of his mouth; no, he is not talking aloud. The man who brought him the fiver, he thinks, with hand pressed to mouth. He says aloud:

"MEMO:
TO: *All branches*
FROM: *Smith, Elizabeth Street*
Dee Bee Smith no longer owes any man anything. He has no debtors."

That will throw them off—they'll believe I've paid a debt with it. Johnie would never put the hammer to me.

Johnie is smiling and lays his arm on Dee Bee's shoulder.

"MEMO:
TO: *Smith, Dee Bee*
FROM: *Leggatt, John*
The Lord chooses strange vessels for his work."

"Hee hee hee hee." Oh yes, it is Johnie, all right. He leans close and winks. "Private memo to Leggatt, John: They will ignore you if you do not envy their respectability."

"Heard of any carpentry jobs open, Dee Bee? Let me know if you do. And, Dee Bee? Have you seen Joe Raven lately?"

Careful! Dee Bee shakes his head, but his lips tighten. Johnie and the tall gray man go away, and he finds his fingers twisting again. He passes a hand over the pocket where his early morning bottle, half full, lies comfortably next to his stomach. He will go round the block and settle somewhere. Ahh, but he cannot go toward the old lumberman's apartment. A choking sense of outrage and despair swells in his throat. Nowhere is safe. More and more Respectables along Bowery and on Elizabeth Street. He knows who waits for the old man. Groping for his bottle, he heads for the nearest doorway.

AHHHHH!

"You bitch! You dirty filthy scabby old bitch!" Proudhomme yanks him into the darkness and viciously pinches his scrotum. "You told them. You told them."

Dee Bee is shaking uncontrollably and cannot speak. Proudhomme's mouth reeks of rotten cheese.

Pinching onto his arm, Proudhomme hauls him back into the sun and maneuvers him toward Elizabeth Street. His long white fingers grasp like talons, and his lipsticked mouth is a parrot's beak. "You sent them away! Joe isn't going to like that, darling. He's been on the wine all night, trying to forget that old man. But it hasn't worked, and so this time I truly think he's going to kill someone. No, not you, you dirty thing. You're not worthy of it. But do you know what he will do with you, darling?"

Dee Bee has gone limp, hangs his head, allows himself to be maneuvered around the corner toward the old man's apartment. But with desperate cunning his mind is ticking off possibilities. He pretends to shut his eyes, but he reads the sidewalk and by its cracks and stains knows exactly where he is.

"He'll have Crook cut just the very tippy-tip of your penis off, darling. That's what he'll do. And make you eat it."

Dee Bee reads the sidewalk and knows he is under DeFord's window. From the corner of his eye, he sees Proudhomme's wrist wriggle upwards and then hears the slow dragging sounds as Raven descends. The metal-ball handle of Raven's ice pick protrudes from under his right sleeve, and his face smiles terribly. At the stoop he twists his upper body and shouts back up the stairwell, "Crook! Get-down here!"

With incredible effort Dee Bee makes his body seem rooted to the pavement until he feels a slight lessening of the white claw on his arm. Behind Raven the lower por-

tions of a man descend like a great primate clothed in dirty khaki.

"Bitch! Bitch! Come back here!"

But Dee Bee has successfully twisted free and is running at an alley. He stumbles, crashes against an ashcan, bolts around the back of the building and finds the boiler-room door. Inside, he drags an empty packing case from the darkest corner and squeezes in. The sound of his wretched breathing seems to fill the room, and it is not until long after it has subsided that he opens his eyes and realizes no one is chasing him.

Now he sips carefully on his bottle of muscatel. They must have decided to go somewhere else. Yes, that's it. For why should they worry about him? They know where the block is. His fingers sooth his patch of dirty silk as he sucks his bottle.

At the very corner of his mind a plan is growing, and he gingerly thinks it first one way, then another, examining it only a bit at a time. Yes, it might work. But he will have to be disguised: shaved, washed, secondhand suit, hat and a pair of cheap dark glasses. The fiver in his pocket will make it all possible. He will escape. In the very middle of the day, disguised as one of Them, he will cross Bowery, head uptown and find another block.

Yes, yes. Shaved, groomed, pressed, polished. Disguised as one of Them.

IV

"I'm to get someone to pick up this package for this pear-shaped guy, see?" Remember said. "Just sit here like we're talking—don't turn round and look at him or nothing. He don't like that."

DeFord said, "You mean he's hired you to keep someone from looking too close at him while you try to contract that someone to fetch a package you've not seen and he's not to look at, and which will no doubt be given over by someone who's trying not to see anything either."

"I'll show you his money if you want. That you can see. It works."

At the dark end of the bar, Leggatt and the bartender were bent over one of Leggatt's canvases, a wineglass on the damp wood between them. The wine seemed to unnerve the bartender, who offered it insistently, then finally drained it himself and laughed at something. I wonder what sort of nonsense they're swapping, DeFord thought.

"See, I don't forget. You wanted a job; I got you one. What you think?"

DeFord stalled by nodding at a woman who had been grimacing throughout Remember's whispered entreaties. Immediately her eyes bulged, purplish lips sagged, and one hand swept to the back of her head as if someone had tapped her with a ball-peen hammer. Clutching a tumbler, she shuffled over, tucking strings of cement-colored hair under an astonishingly clean hat. " 'Lo, doll." Remember turned to his glass, sighed and hung there, shaved head flushing as if he were absorbing port by some silent angry osmosis. "Nice day for a walk round the corner." The woman glared at the door, where three derelicts holding rags swayed on the curb. One leaned toward the traffic, an irreparable mannequin, all joints sprung, beneath what once had been a raincoat. "They're waiting for a wedding. There ought to be a law."

"There is," said Remember. "City Ordinance eight-five-seven-one-one—or is it seven-one-oh, maybe?"

"Fuck you." Then nicely to DeFord: "Isn't it a fine time for a walk, doll?"

"He's signaling how much you want," Remember whispered. "Now he says he'll go ten bucks." Leggatt was still busy, so DeFord said nothing, but he wished there were mirrors backing the bar. Actually, he seldom went into bars, but he remembered the mirrors of each. I suppose I always avoided them, he thought. Not the mirrors, but the men who peeked at themselves until they drank enough to face themselves belligerently, and finally after enough whiskey and talk could gaze peacefully—peacefully? No. Sentimentally. I avoided men who after enough drinks looked into mirrors and felt sentimental about what they found there. Ah, I'm taking things apart like Johnie uses his tongue—a boy with a new penknife. Saints, recluses, maimed, mad, haunted, whipped, tired, sick. The burnt children of the world. This is where they belong, is it not, DeFord? Handsome, but you could get yourself hurt, turning things on their edges. Wasn't it like mirrors? After a while didn't you find what you wanted? And wasn't that good only if you wanted what you needed, or knew what to want? Ah, Johnie, you've started me thinking nonsense already.

"He's signaled twenty bucks now. What you say?" DeFord turned slowly and looked past Remember and beyond Leggatt, where dusty men sat at the bull-pen tables, each with his small wine. When they had entered, a half dozen shuffled over to beg, and they now sat exhausted at the bar front. Alone and apart a pear-shaped man, an exaggerated tic dancing up and down the left side of his cheek, sat behind a glass of stale beer. Deliberately DeFord stared at him and shook his head. "You've done it now." Hunched over his tumbler dregs, Remember shrugged under his loose T-shirt like a bearskin-covered barrel. "I was just—" But Pearshape gestured, and he listed away.

The woman immediately crowded. "Fuck him, doll. He isn't no gentleman, anyway. But I could go for a walk with you. Only couple dollars."

DeFord watched the three on the sidewalk smear rags over a car hood while one approached the driver, hand outstretched. The light changed, a coin was pitched, one scampered from a tangle of horns with a quarter. His partners examined it while he swayed against the lightpost, hands frisking his clothes as if seeking broken bones.

The ringing of the polisher's money on the bar drew the bartender from Leggatt, his towel dragging the wood in a damp slick. Deliberately slow, he slid a fifth of wine to each and gathered their change.

"Only want a pitcher and three glasses."

"You tramps want to spend what you bum front of my

place at some jugshop? Take what I give. I'll throw something out case the Man's seen you." He was slow-faced and contented-looking, but when he smiled, his mouth turned down on gat teeth. He pointed to the knot now standing respectfully watching the polisher's money. "You three. Out!"

"Crissake."

But he was already over his bar, pulling on a heavy mitten, as the have-nots broke for the bull pen. One he caught with a full open hand, then kicked him twice before he could scramble off the floor. Two pressed into a corner, and all three collided with the Man swinging in from the street.

"Those the bunch just come in here?"

"I was throwing them back out."

"Christ. They all look alike to me." The one the bartender had hit was leaning against the doorjamb, so the Man used a night stick on his fingers. "Move on now. Move on."

"Want a drink, Officer? Glass of beer? Hot work." No one spoke while the Man drank, and when he left, the bartender gathered the last of the polisher's change. "For the Man's beer."

"Shit! For cris—"

"What you say?"

". . . nothing. Nothing. I said, 'Nice day, isn't it?' "

"They're all nice days . . . What the hell you lookin' at, Annie? Bring out a price with that handkerchief. You're empty."

"Doll, let's you and me spend it somewhere else." Annie's thick fingers clawed coins.

"Well, goddamn."

"Don't 'goddamn' me, Bert. It's time, and you know it."

The bartender folded his arms. "It's not time."

"You threw those rubbydubs to the Man; you took Ralphie's flop money when all he wanted was a bite—"

"I gave them each a fifth."

"They didn't ask no fifths. And you put the glove to that rubby. And you got no eyes in your head. No, don't pour me a shot. It's time, Bert. You drink it. It's time."

"Oh, for crissake."

"Now it's time."

Bert shrugged, poured, drank. "It tastes like it's time, all right."

DeFord marched down the bar to Leggatt. "I don't want this kind of money." Leggatt continued to examine his painting, although his eyes tallied each wine Bert drank and his foot slid a chair away so Sheriff could sit.

"We came a bit too early. I thought Bert would have hung up his mitten by now. But I have a job for you—"

"Don't think you heard me." DeFord's anger climbed his face in a wash of heat when Remember swayed from Pearshape's table and squeezed between them.

"Hey, Johnie. I got a deal for DeFord here."

"All right! Who's the steadiest hand?" Heads lifted as Bert, face filled with wine, armed a derelict with bottles and pointed him at the bull pen. "For the gentlemen of the rear. Compliments. Pour by the neck. Always a woman by her ears, bottle by its neck."

"He's ripe now," Leggatt said. "Let's get you your job."

"I told you I do not want his money."

"I heard you. But will you take it?"

DeFord slapped the bar with his gloves, then smoothed them as his heart pounded up in his ears. His gloves were supple and worked thin on the palms, yet still durable and tightly stitched. They smelled of elkskin and resin. In the name of God, why had Raven—no, that was not good. I'm supposed to . . . but I won't. You don't want it, but will you take it? If Johnie's right hand can work something his left can't, it's because he hones a double edge to everything. So maybe in this outfit it's my chore to put things back the way they belong. Yes. But nothing's the way it's supposed; you have to account for sag, settling, things drawing in on themselves. For the second time that day he was unsure. I'll ride this out, he thought, folding his gloves into his rear pocket as he looked into Leggatt's eyes.

"Jesus! Johnie, I got thirty bucks for your buddy here—"

"Pearshape, Remember. Pearshape has a pickup to make."

Remember hunched over his empty glass. "So he's a fruitcake, Johnie. He thinks your friend here is a retired cop, but still wants him. I mean he's desperate. But thirty—"

"Why are you trying to find someone for a job you won't take yourself?" asked DeFord.

"I guess I feel sorry for him. He's just come from up river. So I figure he took a four-year smash without telling who'd supplied him. So the deal must have been when he came down they'd fix him a big bag. But now he's shook to pick it up himself. Four years hoeing beans and thinking about the money and it's got him fruity. Anyway, I knew you needed— What's the matter, Johnie? . . . Well, yeah. So I'm lying. I won't take the job, because it's too risky. But I was trying to do a—"

"Did he get as far as you?"

"No, Johnie." Remember's eyes opened wide at DeFord. "The priest there and my head shaved and all when some detective picks up his phone somewhere: 'We just arrested a guy who says he killed that girl last spring, so you better hold up on Baker.' Just that easy. Some guy you'll never know picks up a phone somewhere. That's why you can't let yourself lie. Okay. I don't owe Pearshape nothing. I shouldn've forgotten." His eyes began to water.

"Forget it." Leggatt threw his arm upon the hairy machinery of Remember's back. "Hey. Let me show you something." Remember snuffled, smiled and nodded as Leggatt unrolled a painting. It was a Bowery street, bloodybuckets and porous brick tenements almost imperceptibly unfocused, its people somehow flattened, vaguely fleshed, yet their arrested movements purposeful, compulsively real.

"Elizabeth and Prince," said Remember. "Only . . . I mean it's like you had just peeked round the corner . . . I mean once you actually stepped on it—like once you, say, drank there, maybe flopped there—why, it would never be that way again." He stopped.

"And?" Leggatt soothed.

"Well." Remember sat on his hands. "I mean I wouldn't want to live on a street like that. I mean it's like, were you to step onto the block—well, it's not the sort of block where you could remember very well. You'd have a hard time remembering on that block." He straightened. "I'm sorry, Johnie, but I never liked that block much. And the way you've got it painted here—well, you haven't changed my mind, that's all. But I can see your problem."

"Oh?"

"Sure. I ain't no art critic, but even I can see the thing's all spooky. I mean who'd want to punish himself with something like that on his wall?"

"It did turn out rather well." Leggatt squeezed Remember's shoulders. "Come on up front. We'll buy you a drink."

"Something that works?"

"Something that works."

Flushed and stripped to his T-shirt, Bert gestured munificently at three tumblers. "Wondered when you guys'd decide to be sociable."

"Hey, doll? You come back to take me for that walk?"

"Tell you what we'll do, Bert." Leggatt passed his drink to Remember, who had already swallowed one and seemed to be waiting for something to happen. When it did not, he sipped Leggatt's. "We'll take that shirt you've been intending to get crosstown, and we'll fix it for you. Cleaned, pressed, delivered."

"It's not working."

"Only a buck-fifty, doll. What you say?"

DeFord slid his tumbler to Remember.

"Did I ever show you the old place, Johnie?" Bert passed a photo of a small but well-appointed bar-restaurant. "That's me behind the wood, and that's Eddie on the cash. Eddie's the best, the very best."

Leggatt said, "Eddie will be glad to get his shirt back, won't he?"

"Eddie's all right. Not a thing he wouldn't do for me."

"Doll, you won't be disappointed, 'cause I like you, see? And when I like someone—a buck, what you say?"

Bert wiped the photo carefully. "Those were great times— Hey, counselor! Come in for a bite."

Tanner hesitated on the sidewalk, then came over to the offered tumbler. "Just a taste, Bert. Hello, neighbor. Making money?"

"Not yet. Did I bring you luck?"

"Can't win with one brief, DeFord. Actually, I'm doing fine. Seen God's own number of people."

"You dressed for a wedding, doll?"

Tanner snared his drink with his umbrella, placed his hands near the tumbler, but would not touch it. "Actually, I'm narrowing choices. Hell of a good feeling. But you can't expect something the first—morning. How do I look? I mean around the eyes."

"Ginsburg-Murphy."

The heavy jaw cocked. "Right on course. God, was it only this morning we talked? Feels like last week." He kept dropping his eyes to his hands as if to catch them at something. "In the absolute of course, a man's as young as he feels, but your feet . . . And this damn sen-sen. Been chewing the cursed things all day—morning. Best wash it down." His hands came together around his glass. "DeFord? Here's to you. Negative, Bert. Not another drop. Listen DeFord, about your case against Raven . . ." Tanner drank off half his tumbler and shuddered. "My advice is to leave it be. *Nolo contendere.*" His eyes focused on his glass as if some tiny creature struggled on the surface, drowning. "I represented him. Suit against his employers. Not necessary really, for his union did well by him. But he wanted— Christ knows what he wanted. Or what I wanted. Felt sorry for the dirty thieving bastard, I guess." Tanner drained his glass. "Took his case gratis. Charity of heart. Came down here to straighten him out, and he teased me off the wagon and then robbed me too. I had my chance, you know. Should have told him to kill me right then—but I didn't care—only a few dollars, I thought. So I let the bastard pick me clean. I should have fought. If I had, you see . . . I might have . . . how a man has to feel about working, you see. Honor to yourself. Otherwise, how do you keep at it day after day? So tell me—"

"Hell, Bert," Leggatt was saying, "if you don't want me to take the shirt, just say so."

"Man's talk is man's talk, doll. But I'm still waiting. Tell you what—seventy-five cents. Okay?" Annie reached over Tanner's umbrella and licked out his tumbler.

"I didn't care and it pleased him, so he went away. But then every time I met him on the street, I swear the dirty bastard would go out of his way . . . make me step off into the gutter, you know. If I'd just faced him down . . . or at least packed up and left. But I stayed. I stayed and did nothing, and the damn eels and jellythings came and—"

A hand fell on DeFord's shoulder. Pearshape, left cheek pumping, tipped his pale face toward his table. "You interested in forty bucks, you? Why don't we talk?" His damp spaniel's eyes did not move from DeFord's.

"Bert? Give me something that works, Bert."

"A minute, Remember, for crissake . . . I don't know, Johnie—Eddie's way crosstown."

"So get out of here, neighbor. Let him cash your check. And then pack up and get out."

"Thirty-five cents, then. Because I like you, understand."

"No harm"—he winked—"in talking."

"Sheriff!" DeFord stepped away into the sun, feeling the shock of it as he came out, Sheriff walking behind. At the corner he turned into a beanery, where the short-order cook took one look at him and ran forward, carrying a glass of water. "You'd better lay down in back for a minute, dad."

He swallowed two of his pills, closed his eyes, and when he opened them, the cook was still there. "No, thanks, but if it's not too much trouble, I'll have a cup of black coffee."

◇ ◇ ◇

In a wide saddle heavy with Douglas firs that stirred with the wind two hundred feet above the thick needle duff under his boots, he walked a forest trail scraped to mineral soil, bordered by coarse mattocks of bear grass, and swollen here and there with pustules of bright forest mushrooms. He dreamed and remembered, the dream textured by the memory, yet both threatening nightmare when he tried to judge, as if his mind would permit only the memory while he sought conclusions, reasons, guides. He was on the Mount Hood Wilderness Trail, five miles from his house, resting by a rock slide ripe with vine maple; a Sunday afternoon, at that hour when the forest is without motion, sound, or change. Only the clouds moved, casting shadows over deadfall openings choked with rhododendron, juniper, and salal. He was sitting on the edge of a thousand square miles of trackless forest enmeshed by a series of ridge paths—part blazed lines, part hogbacks, mostly game trails; sitting alone in the trackless silence when he looked into the shadows and saw a man watching him.

When he tried to understand, the forest darkened, while the man, motionless as a dry stump, seemed to swell and advance. He saw himself raise his hand and the man's head dip; then he was walking, only doubting at that instant he passed from bright sun into the great trees' shadows and saw behind the man what seemed a sleeping horse, head resting between an arch of polished greasewood. "Hiking?" the man said. The horse became a dead elk, antler tips almost as far apart as the man was tall. "Been hunting?" DeFord asked. "On the reservation," the man answered. Still he did not move, and DeFord realized he waited a release. Of course! "The season is always open on the reservation, isn't it?" he said. "My wife's people can always hunt. But only on the reservation," the man replied. All right, DeFord thought. I don't care where or when you hunt, mister. The man smiled, nodded, and began to dress out his bull. He worked the hide off quickly with a skinning knife, then went to his packboard for a hatchet, small folding saw, rope, and cheesecloth. DeFord said nothing but helped quarter the animal and hoist the heavy sections off the ground. In two hours, when they were finished, the man said, "Come back after dark and pack out whatever you want." DeFord shook his head. "How much will he weigh?" The man smiled. "One thousand, maybe eleven hundred." He folded the hide, rolled it, and lashed it to his packboard. "I'll be back tonight—with friends. Nice and cool with a good moon on the ridges. Have him out by morning. Won't lose a chop, unless the government men are here. Then we'll lose it all." He straightened and not without difficulty swung into his pack. "And the government men will have to bury it. Lots of roots, rocks. Hard work." He picked up his rifle and smiled. "Unless you tell them yourself," DeFord said, "there won't be anybody here waiting for you tonight." The man nodded. "You change your mind, come back and take what you can carry. Tastes like beef." "Only better," DeFord said. The man grinned. "Only better." DeFord shook his head. "It's not elk season for me." He started back, the man following, and when they came to the ridge line where the trail dropped along the main drainage, the man said, "You walk this ridge with me for half a hour, I'll show you something."

Now half asleep, DeFord tried to will the poacher to speak, to confess how long he had known of the airplane. Had he really known for all of ten years, and did he feel it was the land's secret, not his to tell, and how could he have left the pilot undiscovered for so long, and— But under his judgments the dream became a nightmare, so he went silently with the poacher along the ridge and down to a saddle of rhododendron and greasewood. "He came in here," the poacher said, "but he was moving too fast and bellied under the timber. Maybe that's why they never found him. Maybe they never looked."

The wreckage was two hundred yards into the timber,

strewn among the giant trees like great rusted leaves, but the fuselage was intact: a long rusted boiler enveloped in knots of rhododendron. The pilot's skeleton sat upright under a tree, sunken to its pelvis in the duff, so bleached and dry it seemed the remains of some elaborate kite, uniform and leather jacket mere strips of tissue. Somehow to DeFord the rusted pistol and its eight blackened cartridges on the rock seemed more real than the wreckage, the skeleton, the very woods itself. Both weapon and spent shells lay undisturbed, untouched by the vines and brush that had virtually swallowed the rest. Only the bone pistol grips showed time: white, cracked, their edges gnawed by rodents. DeFord stared, but when he tried to understand how the poacher could have left the pilot so long, could have abandoned him, the memory disintegrated. He himself became the pilot, his legs broken, his signals nothing more than eight dull flat protests absorbed by the million silent trees. And he saw himself alive when the poacher first came. And he saw himself— No, no, he thought. It is not the dying—it is being alone, it is being abandoned.

"Round here they used to train their pilots back in nineteen and forty, nineteen and forty-one."

So now it is what? DeFord thought. Almost twenty years.

"I was trapping then. Lining this whole ridge. And my wife's people too. It was where we worked. The government would have known we was in here." The poacher squatted, his rifle a tripod to his heels, and braced his head on his wrist so the weight of the hide rested mostly on the rifle. "They had seasons on fur. Limits and licenses. Everything. They would have sent us all down the road the hell out of this country."

But twenty years. Without a grave for twenty years.

The poacher leaned more heavily on his rifle, staring

at the spent cartridges. "He didn't save one for himself. That's what I can't read. You'd think they would've told a man that." He laughed carefully. "He must have thought he was just over the ridge from somebody's yard. All broke to hell in some farmer's wood lot."

"No," DeFord said, "he knew. But he knew someone would find him someday, too. Somebody would want to know how he died. His wife maybe."

The poacher straightened and turned toward the ridge above the saddle. "We'll go up same way we dropped down so tomorrow you can bring the government to their man without swimming through the brush. They wouldn't know better themselves." On the ridge he rested again on his rifle.

"You've known for fifteen years at least. Why do you want them now?"

"He's been down there long enough, I guess. Here, help me shift this hide. Your trail is just other side that snag."

"Wait! Suppose I tell them you've known?"

"I figure you won't. It's all done now. The range been closed since nineteen and thirty. Big men got everything —little men got out. Price on fur's not even a joke. The rich women's men pay plenty, but the man who salts it never sees nothing. It's all done now. You know. I can tell you know. So you won't say nothing."

DeFord wanted to cry, "Wait!" But the memory of the poacher's mad eyes distorted until, in his dream, he was again in the saddle. Again with the rusted metal sheets curled in the shadows of the great trees.

Alone. Abandoned.

V

"There they are: every beast too slow for the ark—pterodactyls, coelacanths, spiny armadillos. All the lesser extinct."

In a pale sky burned of clouds, DeFord guessed the sun close to one o'clock. "How long did you let me rest, Johnie?"

"Three hours. It took almost an hour to find you—then I saw Sheriff waiting in the alley and remembered that cook has a bunk in back." Ahead at the Bowery Mission a sullen queue waited for compulsory service and free soup.

Ahh, DeFord thought. Three hours. It comforted and at the same time almost angered him. So I am not alone. I am beholden more than I would have it. "Beholden": the word seemed a judgment. Lately, especially in the months since his heart attack, DeFord surprised himself using his father's style. I am the last of an old family, he thought. And that is as sentimental as gutting yourself full of whiskey so you can come to peace with your face in a bar mirror. But if you think it without feeling sorry, it won't slip to sentiment. And more so, if you are gentle with such a truth and don't ride more work out than it's got the wind for, then maybe you won't have such dreams and break a sweat in the midday. He had come East, he thought cautiously, because he was the last of an old family. And because, he could admit, now the habit of his heart was in question and—yes, damnit—now he was at last tied down with no power to cut loose and run. He had come East because he hoped to find, or simply to glimpse, just what had kept him going it alone so long. How many places did I homestead in my twenties, anyway? And my thirties, how many places did I put up for other folks? And what was I working at and looking for in my forties made it so flat impossible to find a woman I could settle in with? Then ten, a dozen years building the big tract places—nothing more than homesteading again with all that made homesteading worth the while tamed and prefabbed out. And since I built the last place of my own, why did I have to come all the Christ's way back where the whole chore started three-hundred-odd years ago? Now I've seen the last DeFord grave shy of my own, all I know is whatever we were looking for other than steady wages and a full deep-freeze, we never got a piece of, not since the first of us set foot in the New York colony. If I know anything, DeFord thought, suddenly realizing he was furious, flat absolutely furious with himself, Leggatt, Tanner, Codgers, the city itself—because it was becoming apparent no friends, acquaintances or paid public servants, consequently no help, advice or duty, would keep Joe Raven from him, much less indicate why Raven had seized upon him in the first place—if I know anything, it's whatever a goddamned DeFord expected beyond a reasonably full pantry, this country never was able to generate. Or else we worked ourselves into a twenty-two-inch collar and size-six hat and whatever it was was too complicated for such dull machinery to remember, or we bred ourselves so tight-lipped we couldn't allow ourselves to mention it. And that information alone, aside from brute company, was all DeFord could possibly see he might offer for Leggatt's already three hours and more of neighborly attention.

And so he said only, "I appreciate your letting me sleep. I have to stop by my clinic sometime today, and the rest will have set me better."

Leggatt muttered it off: "Nothing. Besides, I was sucking up coffee, trying to get up enough balls to stop by my gallery. We'll swing by your clinic on the way to Codgers' place."

"Before or after your gallery?"

"I'm not as nervy as I thought. The hell with my gallery."

Ah, DeFord thought. Perhaps there is something I can swap him, then. "I've never been to an art gallery," he said. And when Leggatt did not answer: "Someday you'll have to take me—that is, when you feel a bit more bullish." Leggatt pursed his lips. "How soon do you imagine your neck will be swollen up big enough—"

"Okay, for crissake," muttered Leggatt. "If you can make the clinic, I can make my fucking gallery."

"I don't want to impose—"

"Then stop grinning. Clinic, gallery, dinner at Codgers' place. By then the laundry will have finished Eddie's shirt, and I'll run it crosstown for you and meet you—"

"So you took the job. All right. But I'll make the trip with it."

"Ha." Leggatt threw his arm over DeFord's shoulders and squeezed. "How will you spend your five dollars? Wheat germ and honey?"

"Maybe I'll buy you a drink of good bourbon, Johnie." DeFord turned away, suddenly shy. A man, he thought, a man must hold himself up alone, not be held up by others. But the advice seemed meaningless, and he wondered: Has he embraced me out of love of life or love of me? He wanted to ask if Leggatt had worried for him, but he feared some extravagant answer, so he thought: All right then, let it be. It's true. I am afraid to know.

"No. No. No bourbon." Leggatt dropped his arm and walked with head down, hands jammed into rear pockets. "No bourbon. No." He brightened as they came to the mission and its queue waiting for soup. "Ignore me, DeFord. I'm entering a new age with the discovery my worst is actually the best in me. Or is it"—he touched DeFord's elbow and drew him close—"my best that is the worst in me?"

"It's your nonsense gets the better of you."

"Nonsense? My nonsense, nonsense? Listen, man is constantly rediscovering himself, returning home as it were. Well, I tried a shortcut, got lost and had to live a good many nights in the streets." Leggatt held DeFord's elbow as he maneuvered through the queue of exhausted men. "Here you stand among the extinct in the last place they might adapt. If not—there is the East River. And if so—there is still the river."

They were deep among the mission men, answering with empty hands the outstretched palms, and DeFord saw that Leggatt was studying him, tallying his reactions. Perhaps his nonsense isn't nonsense after all, DeFord thought. But it's an imposition, and just about half dangerous, I'd bet. "There are a lot of places. This is big country."

"You talk like a man who's paid his own way for a long time, DeFord. But there are a lot of different markets too. And products."

Fair enough, thought DeFord. I'll play poker with you. I've the time. "What did you do before you came to live over the river?"

"River," Leggatt corrected. "You have to say it with the prayerful finality of an overly long and tedious bus trip." He jammed his hands into his pockets. "I was a victim."

DeFord let it lie for a while, then thought: All right, my move I guess. "Of what?"

"My country."

"How so?"

"I believed things. I was democratic. Square. Stupid even. To this day I'm not really very bright."

"What things?"

Leggatt grinned and squeezed DeFord's biceps. "Listen. I once saw a pig swallow a rattlesnake. Swuzzled like a living noodle. Absolutely harmless, as the venom was digested, not savored. Show, don't tell. Entertainment. You see? If I were an entertainer, I'd elaborate my adventures as a fornicator just before I fled to the river three years ago. Twelve different women. Twelve consecutive days. What do you think of that, DeFord?"

"If you say so, I believe."

"It's a lie. The truth was: eleven were unbelievably easy, and the last showed me I had become common, stupid. From the moment my final ploy failed to bed her, I was drunk with freedom from sex. So I confessed the contest as we waited for the cab to take her home. 'Eleven?' she asked. 'Never mind, cabbie!' she said. And a victim to my vacuous contest, I followed her snapping tail back to my apartment. 'Tell me if that wasn't the very best,' she whispered when she'd finished with me. 'Wasn't it?' And that, DeFord, was the last time I was so democratic as to believe every idea should be judged. The last time I allowed my body to use me. The last of a whole nest of snakes I swuzzled. Next day I flopped at the Three Lions. I, a pair of remittance men from two of the better families in the city, and a sociologist who came down to research a paper and got hooked on port wine were the only ones who rented by the month. The sociologist lasted one winter, then poured himself under a subway. Poor bastard. For years he had wound himself up and ticked all day, giving the hour to the minute. But the poor son of a bitch never realized if he didn't keep rewinding himself, his key would corrode, his mainspring would snicker, and some slow-turning swamp of an afternoon he wouldn't be able to leave Elizabeth Street. The remittance men had it made—their weekly check removed all responsibility. 'Here's some money to stay down there and drink yourself to death and leave us alone, you hear. Love, Mother/Dad/Brother/Sis.' My check was monthly, so I had to be more disciplined. Impossible to be a decent, sniveling, silent victim when you've got to be disciplined. It's like falling in love or taking a job. It keeps you straight. Patriotic. But patriotism doesn't interest you? I thought not. Are you the sort who feels whenever there is a government anywhere, he is against it?"

DeFord smiled. "No. But I met a man that breed. He was poaching elk." It was work, listening to Leggatt. It was an imposition. It was as if you thought you knew all about life in your own backyard and then one day went to move an old wagon hub and saw a handful of strange, ugly and beautiful creatures slither out of the sun, drawing themselves deep into the sod of your own paid-for and hand-built place. But he kept on with his poker game, knowing somehow that if he didn't draw out Leggatt now, he might not have another chance. And he did not want to be alone. "So you were a remittance man yourself?"

"There is remitted to me, once a month, a check for seventy-six dollars and forty-three cents. It's from We the People. Because of certain outrages—mostly my diarrhea of the mouth—my government decided I had become exempt. Schizophrenic. It was a shame, really. I was a nice, almost bright boy, they thought—and I'd swallowed all the headcheese of American education: the myths, the heroes, the facts, the common unambitious twaddle, the truths, the lies—but just as they were squeezing the last of my Army duty out of me, something went wrong. And in the process of declaring me exempt, they decided where it took the average guy so much time to filch so much money from his neighbor, it would take me twice as long, and they really ought to be nice guys and help me out. So I'm on permanent one-half disability compensation."

"And you came down here to paint?"

"I came down here to drink. My American apprenticeship is over: little boy, student, soldier, painter, fornicator, drunk. Unfortunately, I've always liked painting. Never been able to forget the simplicity of my childhood toys: blocks, crayons, storybooks. Worse, I get raging hangovers, leaving me useless for weeks. So I failed as a drunk." Leggatt tucked his fist under his arm and dropped one shoulder. "Failed as fornicator because I thought I was fucking, whereas I was being fucked." His other fist burrowed in his armpit, his neck went limp, head lolled, and DeFord was walking with a babbling cripple. "See the broken apprentice who failed soldiery by being neither scared enough of Them or Us, failed as student by learning neither to fuck or fight, failed as little boy by— How do you fail as a little boy, DeFord?"

"You left out the painting." He'd had enough of poker now. Leggatt held too many wild cards.

"I've failed only to make it pay. Which isn't anything new." He watched DeFord take his work gloves from his pocket, pull at them, smooth, fold them. "You're probably thinking nothing's easy." He grinned when DeFord slapped the gloves on his thigh and returned them to his hip. "Thought so. Well, when we get to my brother's gallery and you see the work of this city's newest genius, with whom I exhibit, you'll see just how wrong you are."

"And those notes you asked me to write?" DeFord tried at the poker game, but it did not come. He felt he was being used. He felt strangely alone, as if some old habit, some partner-to-partner bantering defense, had broken down. The game was too rich. He was too old for new friendships. No, it was flat exactly the other direction. He needed the game. He needed Leggatt. He needed not to lose anything more that day. "Those notes are meant for this new genius?"

"Yes. You see it's not Kreplun's success I envy. It's having to starve while I watch it. So I thought I'd needle Kreplun a bit. Then I decided the hell with it, it's too dangerous. But you were right, starting the business of having a swollen enough neck. I don't have to take myself so seriously, least of all Kreplun. Climbing that fucking ladder was serious enough business for the day."

So it frightens him. The knowledge made DeFord feel better. Less used. And that was maybe just what Codgers wanted. Leggatt would be scared and he less used. No. No. I'm jumping myself. It's getting too rich again. "And what of Codgers?"

"Codgers?" Leggatt buried his hands in his rear pockets and grinned. "Great gods! If I lower the skrim of a week's absence from the old monkey, I see him a grizzled, nearly juiceless homunculus, chattering from concept to concept at the dribbling headwaters of the philosophical life. Frankly, I disliked him for quite a while because I was no match for him. Then I stopped taking myself so seriously, and we got along famously. You have to learn Codgers. As you would learn an old and formidable . . . anything old and formidable."

A merchant, two umbrellas over his arm, a pocket oozing glasses and watchbands, waved at Leggatt, and he released DeFord. "Hello, McMitchell. How's the market?"

"Unkempt." McMitchell, face and hands tanned a golden mahogany, plunged one fist into a shopping bag, exposing a forearm the color of a frog's underbelly. He held out a small yellow square. "Wall-la! This one—this one was not only unkempt, but incohanted. Still, he said it was honorary."

Leggatt held the pin to the sun. "Sigma Psi. It's what he said. Unkempt, you say?"

"Incohanted too, Johnie."

"Incoherent."

"Yeah? Gave a small pitcher for it." DeFord stared at his umbrellas. "Want one?" DeFord shook his head. "This one"—McMitchell brandished Tanner's thin silk—"this one was still quite inchoate."

"The damn, damn fool," DeFord snapped. The sight of Tanner's umbrella brought a remorse much like his morning feeling of nakedness, and he sensed an inexplicable sadness, a sadness so oppressing in the dry midday glare he felt somehow betrayed. And at the same time ashamed.

Leggatt looked at him; his eyes went brittle and he turned away. "Coherent."

"Yeah . . . Real honorary you say, Johnie? If it's honorary I get twice the price of its gold. From a guy crosstown. He's a real 'centric."

"Why don't you scout uptown pawnshops?"

McMitchell shook his mahogany face. "I couldn't do that, Johnie. He only wants the honoraries I pick up here. That's the deal. So I couldn't go uptown. Say, nice jacket —give you two bucks."

"McMitchell, I could get twice that."

"Not down here. We stick together. Clean jacket—this week's top two bucks. But I'll tip you: the give is upping to four next month so's we can load for the winter."

"When you'll sell for eight and buy for a dollar."

"Ah, Johnie. We'll buy for three pitchers. Sounds better now, don't it?"

"You know, McMitchell"—Leggatt studied the gutter with deep respect—"each time we meet, I rediscover the eternal rift between those who fart and those who have noses."

"It's a matter of honor, isn't it?"

"Some people carry their own toilet paper in this world. And there are those who don't."

McMitchell sucked out his chest. "We stick together, all right."

"In these days it's a rare and demanding thing."

"Times have changed." McMitchell looked up and down Bowery with soft damp eyes. "Back before they tore down the El—"

"Golden days, McMitchell. Golden days."

"Yeah. But we've always stuck together. Well, see you around, Johnie. Hang tough."

They walked north toward Great Jones Street, Leggatt nodding to shuffling men, DeFord behind, Sheriff between. DeFord guessed that with the rest Leggatt allowed him, he had just a doe's hair better than even chance Raven would not show on his examination. Then with a bit more luck—no, he did not trust luck for himself; he trusted habit, his curse. If his habits held, he would be back in Oregon before the snow closed the high country; at latest for the spring mulching of his vegetable garden. He wondered whether it would be the younger doctor who, when he worked his Saturday charity, sat upon his desk a picture of his pretty children and prettier wife so the mission men might reflect upon the rewards of temperance, or his own older doctor, who kept a half dozen nails in a Mason jar of fresh cheap sauterne, the heads labeled with date of submersion, the tips in stages of leprous decay. If Raven had made a difference already, he hoped his own doctor determined it. When he started with the clinic, he had placed by the jar of rotting nails his seed catalogs—Burpees, Ferris, the lot—his own measure of time. And his doctor took them up, turning past vegetables and fruits to the roses. He envied DeFord the Oregon coast's rainy gentle winters. Once, he admitted, after a convention in Oregon during the Portland Rose Festival, he returned to his Long Island house and for a week could not look into his own rose garden. DeFord countered by lamenting the difficulties of ripening big beefsteak tomatoes on the Cascade slopes and how he had to build reflector backings in September. His doctor suggested rock mulch to hold in the heat, and DeFord said he would try it. Did the doctor ever bury rusted metal by his rose roots to deepen their color? The doctor had read of it when he was younger and had scoffed. But coming from an Oregon man, he'd test it, and thanks.

DeFord understood that he was subject to another attack, but if the valve repaired as expected, it could very well be some other damn organ that got him. Generally speaking, his doctor stated, putting it quite roughly: if a man's heart held and he did not pick up cancer, why, he had a good chance of living a long, long time. "You have a marvelous machine here, Mr. DeFord," the doctor said, bending over his wide, gently freckled back, moving the cool ear of the stethoscope past the slack but still formidable biceps and laying it in the lower right triangle of grizzled chest hair, where the muscle hung loose and heavy. "If our pump patching takes as it should, it could carry you a long way yet."

But it was not his doctor today. While Leggatt waited in the street with Sheriff, who shied at the odor of the clinic and crept to Leggatt for the first time, DeFord was examined by the younger doctor. "Coming slowly, avoid strain, plenty of rest and"—the man busied himself with a pencil—"I'll be taking your case from now on." DeFord did not move. "It was not his heart," the young doctor said. "And there is no pain. But the exploration showed it as terminal . . . I'll see you in another week, DeFord. You must understand now, it has nothing to do with his heart."

"Oh, I understand, mister. I understand." His doctor had told him that even though cancer had taken his grandfather, mother and then an uncle, he still believed he would see the day they could cure it. Well, he hadn't.

Back in the street DeFord said nothing, though Leggatt was extravagantly impatient and finally challenged, "We can pass up my gallery trip and go straight to Codgers' digs."

"No." DeFord was still angry. He was tired of having things slip away. I waited too long before I came back East, and it takes a different brand of nerve. But that's my road. And I shouldn't go hard on Johnie because he's younger, or an Eastern boy, or simply not my kind of man. And maybe he is, he thought quickly, just as quickly dismissing it as worthless. "No, Johnie, I'm fine. And we should get your gallery chore done. It's not much of a swap, but it will make me feel better."

"Okay," said Leggatt, as if the word were "bullshit." And then "Okay, why not?" as if he had changed his mind. They walked east, south, east again until DeFord was lost, but Sheriff seemed increasingly confident in the fix of his scent.

"Coyote with a mile of fence post and fifty gallons of pee," said DeFord.

"Sheriff and I have something in common, all right," Leggatt muttered. And when DeFord questioned: "We're surfacing into the East Village. A flank of the scene I deserted three years ago." He bent and petted Sheriff. "What poor son of a bitch did you track out of here to Elizabeth Street? Or did you leave on your own? Interesting theory, DeFord. Why did your dog leave this for Bowery? Now I came because I'm a hick. Fishing for eels under my bridge the other night, I finally accepted I'm a hick. I lack a sense of play, a certain sophistication." He straightened, shook his wrists above his head as if to break a fit of epilepsy, and then flung them to his sides. "There are a few thick-skinned bastards doing decent work here—but the bulk are honest-to-God free American citizenry who could do something decent or honorable but have elected, DeFord, have actually chosen, to become the swuzzlingest pack of swine extant. They— You see, DeFord? I'm a hick. I take it seriously. I embarrass people. Why can't I grow up? Why can't I stop making poor mouth?" He grinned and waved his arms. "So I escaped. I went exempt. Went east to the river. You went west to the ocean. Tell me, DeFord, just what the hell do you have out there?"

"A house. A few acres. Some outbuildings—" The fact of his doctor's cancer was getting through to him, and he thought if he could list his few solid, well-run possessions, the litany might bring a calm. Suddenly he realized he had forgotten to wrap old blankets around his freezer, and in his now—what?—three months' absence, his electric bill would be a good ten, fifteen dollars stouter than it might. He tried to remember just what lay in his freezer and if any of it would be touched with lockerburn. Forty-odd pounds of good buck meat steaked and wrapped and two half-saddles and probably three feet of backstrap—

Leggatt had started up again, still marveling over some

young man's philosophy or another, so DeFord let him run, his own mind ticking off his larder.

"There are other escapes: filching money, knitting bones, going to war, making bombs. Man is the definitive sore loser, yes? Give him a Pasteur or Salk, and he's lavish with gratitude. A Von Braun or Oppenheimer, and he wants to impound the monster's Chemo-set and make him stand in a corner."

Then the heart and kidneys of that little forked-horn I cracked last summer—have to get to those right way, make a pie of it with bacon all over the top and meadow mushrooms. Must have three or four cartons of wild mushrooms left—freeze up all right, better than drying them. And a pair of nice silver salmon, steaked and frozen in ice to keep from burning. And a dozen cartons of sea-run cutthroat trout. Four or five mallard ducks—

"Notice my concern with current events? Living over the river has gotten my pecker up. Which is no doubt why Codgers prescribed it. Clever old monkey. Here I thought he was a friend, and the old mummer turns right around and tries to help me."

—and three black Brant geese. No, he'd swapped the Brant for some antelope meat and broiled that when a town friend came out to visit. And a quarter of grass-fed beef with just a little grain to marble it off. Some bear meat a friend had given him—made the best stew he ever ate—

"Did I ever tell you the first thing the old monkey said to me about my painting? He peered over my shoulder while I was at work and squeaked, 'Sometimes in a very remarkable man one finds only a mediocre artist, but in you, Johnie, this is not true.' I'm still trying to fathom just what the hell he meant by it."

—six pints of blue mussel meat—a mess of Dungeness

crabs, cooked and frozen whole—some fine thick halibut steaks—

"Christ, DeFord, what are you grimacing at?"

DeFord swallowed. "What?" He swallowed again. "Oh. Guess I'm just hungry, that's all."

◇ ◇ ◇

A series of small cupboardlike rooms extended from a main room whose long west wall was stripped to adobe-size brick painted white. In a large fireplace an offering of pressed sawdust burned slowly, without smoke, eaten to ash from within. No one room was level with another, but connected by short narrow stairs hung with black netting no doubt serving as a warning or handhold, but somehow suggesting the castings of a large spider. Prospective buyers ambled up and down, pressing in on each other toward a small bar in the center of the large room.

Kreplun had plunged among his buyers; DeFord saw flashes of his fleshtone nylon shirt, plastic ascot, the aspirin-colored surveyor's vest abulge with slide rules, hand lenses, drafting tools, graph papers—which he used from time to time, as if assessing the warp and sag of his riotous bathmat and kitchen-sink paintings. Leggatt led through the exhibition rooms, face controlled, feet impatient, and was opening a door marked "Private" when he hesitated, said, "Well, why not?" and drew DeFord into a small room where two of Kreplun's monuments were propped back to back on a small revolving table, their porcelain surfaces languorously offering hors d'oeuvres.

Leggatt pointed to a painting of his own: partially razed tenement apartments, interiors trapping the sun in a mottle of bricks, holes and painted walls; in the foreground a field of rubble, stripped and leveled as if awaiting a seeding. "Nearly sold that. The creature who specked it returned the damn thing. Too specific, too disturbing. Well, she won't find her Kreplun too disturbing. In two weeks it will disappear right into the wall. Anyway, thought someone might have picked it up. There's the type." He gestured toward four of Kreplun's admirers—sleek women, with hair in the style of the late President's wife, clothes identically cut, wearing the same tall fur hats and carrying leather handbags the size of small garbage cans. They so perfectly resembled each other that DeFord thought for a moment they might be part of the display.

DeFord was embarrassed by it all. Everything was rich: the smells were all wrong. No. It was rather that he could not understand the process. Workshops he knew, and yards, mills, landings—but marketplaces left too much out. It was a form of progress beyond his experience. "How does he do it?" DeFord asked, staring up over a desk where one of Kreplun's oils hung limp from the wall like a sour and unfleshed calf hide.

"Intuition."

"You mean luck?"

"Not only." Leggatt rinsed two mugs while DeFord set up the coffee. "It's a marriage—correction, an orgy—between good seasoned technique, a hot piece of luck and brass balls. The actual process is intuition. It's much like watching a cat leap an alley. See it gather and regather its footing, knead, reknead, twitch, feint until in such a frenzy of adrenaline and goosiness—it launches! If successful, the world is extended by another roof. If not, you buy another cat. Kreplun works that way: after brooding thoughtlessly, half asphyxiated with the mindless feel of it, he launches himself at unstretched canvas—more bounce when he lands—and begins to daub."

"He's learned to keep his mouth tight, then."

"But you know, DeFord, I sense his histrionics are losing their hold on the usual crowd. Inevitable. His work is a rather imaginative July Fourth display, and one can ponder just so many Roman candles and flower bursts. Don't misunderstand. I'm not optimistic for my own work. But I do sense Kreplun hopping on the lip of a giant discovery, a final bang to draw the last ooooh-ahhhh and leave this season's art lovers blinded to silence, desperately pumping visual purple back into their gasping retinas as the cash registers chorus a timpani of applause."

Well, it was none of his business, DeFord thought. But it was—he set the pot to boil and sat on the counter, holding his boot heels out from the cupboard—it was . . . He counted his habit. He was old again. Now. Because he wanted to accept that Leggatt was foolish, boyish, not yet a full man. But looking across forty-odd years, he guessed Leggatt was tall enough. Yes, I moved on. And Johnie stayed. So it's not for me to judge. And the hate Leggatt had flung him? That had been an accident; his affection for Leggatt forced truth past pride. The truth was, Leggatt had flung hate as a man might the tool with which he mashed his thumb. You had to expect such accidents whenever you teamed. Two men together always involved each other in their accidents. "Then you won't exhibit with him again?"

Leggatt said nothing, merely went to the refrigerator, dropped an ice cube into his coffee and watched it disappear. Then he drained the cup and looked up with the same suggestion of madness-ambition he had brought all the terrible way up from the river that morning. "The question seems to be: How much of your ass will you sell to the pigs? But that's my bag, DeFord. And now I'll go look for my brother, thank you."

As DeFord sipped hot, boiling tonguefuls, his contentment shed its threat of sentiment. He distrusted sentiment; for him it always dropped sickeningly to anger and pain. Since the girl in Craig—which had been a mistake, he had no doubt of that—a dozen times he might have settled into some woman's kitchen, but something came along—an offer for more interesting work, an obsession to change country, change a mountainside for dryland desert, change rented valley cottage for rented ocean bungalow. Once he worked seven weeks of eighteen-hour days to honor a handshake contract on twelve units in a Bakersfield motel, then with his check wet, bused to Plymouth, Washington, where the trickiest sections of the McNary Dam were going over Hood River. From the porch of a borrowed shack, he watched steel inch stubbornly over the gorge after incredible attacks by a battalion of laborers. And he had been drawn into it, of course—assisting timber inspection of lighter forms. To be part of the work. The evening before east and west sections linked, it rained hard without warning. Under arc lamps the pulled crews watched the I beams stretched on their temporary bolts, lacking thirty feet to clasp but trembling under sheets of water. The day before, the engineers had ordered off paint crews despite mounting indignation: the paint crews were at such a pitch of competition with iron monkeys and riveters they would have sprayed bare air for a linkup of their own, but they were pulled so the last sections might be lighter by a few tons of red lead. Whether that had saved it, no one would ever know, but when the storm front stabilized and the linkup was made, the gunmen and buckerups lacked but three sixteenths of an inch perfect fit to the rivet holes.

DeFord cashed in when the finishing started. None of it had been his line, and patching the borrowed shack tempted him to put his hands to his own craft. Perhaps it was also the taste of salt flats in the gorge's west winds. So he went to Nestucca Bay for some Chinook fishing. Or was it . . . ? Forgotten.

Yes, leaving the girl in Craig had been a mistake. By the

time he accepted it, the wandering had seized him. Wandering? Only the DeFord promise the country was big enough. And perhaps that was wrought of DeFord anger when DeFords learned that no matter how big the land, its people were never so big. Whatever, his work and the land satisfied. Except when he was tired or stuffed with some woman's food or both, and began to feel sorry he could not come home to such every night. Something had always interfered: people, he guessed. People would do the damnedest things: throw up some sloppy box of a house somewhere and run themselves to death in smiling, chattering circles, trying to outwit their neighbors. And join things? Good bearded Jesus. Clubs, legions, associations, committees, lodges, funds, organizations, halls, churches. He swallowed a full slug of the coffee. Hell, the people were all good people; it was their blubbering he could not abide. Yes, he might have found a good woman had he really tried. The country was big enough for that too. Barely.

No, there had been something else as well. Maybe he'd started moving around too early. The country was easy for that. You kept moving about; you left houses, cabinets, chairs, tables behind—how many cars had he owned? How many pickups had he driven out? How many tons of metal, machinery, wood, stone, glass, chemicals—things—had he left behind? All different, used, worn, changed, broken, never again the same, discarded. Abandoned . . . Am-er-ik-ka, he sounded to himself, sensing the primitive sound of it. America, it was incredible! His mind roared in his skull, picking and nudging. I won't think about it, he resolved, and found a toilet, where he lightened himself of coffee and washed up. Rising from the water, he saw his face rather haggard and glassy in the mirror. "You look like eight miles of bad road, DeFord," he said aloud.

Leggatt entered, palmed water over his face and studied

him. "Couldn't find my brother. Kreplun's fled too. Get the feeling whatever Frank's set up for himself must be big bullshit—even for him. Wish to hell we weren't so broke. Prefer to stay out of his way. Can't win them all, though." He studied DeFord. "Just what the hell are you thinking about, DeFord?"

"How much like you I'm beginning to sound."

"It's the atmosphere." Leggatt rubbed himself dry, folded the towel and made a few passes through his hair with his fingers. "You'd better cut it out, though. It's all right psychologically—but all wrong dramatically."

◇ ◇ ◇

They retraced to Bowery, Sheriff diligently remaking his scent where it failed reexamination. Nothing was said until the corner of Houston, where across the street DeFord saw Joe Raven armed with a broomstick, batting old tennis balls over a partially cleared lot. Some teen-agers caught, while to the side of the backstop Proudhomme deflected returns with his feet before passing them on.

"Johnie?"

"Yes, it's Joe. And that thing sitting there is Crook."

"I'm going to talk with them."

"I'll give you some damn good reasons why you shouldn't."

Raven flipped a ball, batted it viciously, and DeFord hesitated.

"Joe's broke, for one. And he's mean sober, for another."

Raven lined one, shouted derisive encouragement; the teen-agers answered and Raven waved. How boyish he is, how shameless, DeFord thought. Then Raven dragged his legs, and he felt a sour mixture of terror and pity.

Leggatt gestured as if to take his arm, but did not. "It would be better to wait till he comes by a little money and

some wine—not too much, though. And we have some money as well."

"Do you think I'd buy back my check?"

"You may have to."

"Nonsense." He started across the street.

"You're a goddamn old fool, DeFord."

DeFord stopped but could not speak. When he wet his lips the gesture seemed stupid, hopeless.

"I'm sorry I said that."

"Doesn't matter."

"No. Listen, I am sorry. I'm sorry I said that. Jesus Christ, DeFord." Leggatt spread his arms, dropped them and hid his hands as DeFord mounted the curb. "At least have a talk with Codgers."

"All right, Johnie. I'll give that far." Raven shouted, lashed a grounder and pounded rubble as Proudhomme fumbled and Crook teased. "But I won't buy it back."

VI

"Now the hound, now the hare, Mr. DeFord." Codgers hopped between a small stove and a series of kitchen cabinets crowded in one corner of his loft, covering a meat board with onions, garlic, fruit, bottles and canisters. Under a thin turtleneck sweater, his bony shoulders swayed above baggy trousers. "One should be concerned only with the making of money or watches; then there would never be life enough to finish. But some things I do not try to understand. I accept." He sliced the onions carefully, to thin, tapering wedges. "Something always takes shape when I stare into the depths of myself long enough and have the discipline to ignore the dreams I project there. And were you to stare into yourself or Joe Raven, you too would see something. You would see yourself and Joe Raven staring back." Codgers shaved onions with quick precision while a larded skillet sent blue smoke

to the skylight. "Great things fall to great, the depths are revealed to the profound, thrills and refinements to the refined, and—everything strange to the estranged." His hand passed among bottles and canisters, pitching spices to the hot fat. Cloves, chilies and cinnamon bark curled their incense to the room. When they had been leached of flavor, Codgers seared the chicken, laid it aside and browned his mountain of onions in the spiced oil. Almost under his feet, Sheriff sat swallowing repeatedly. "Haven't you fed that animal yet? . . . Here." He snatched a wad of hamburger from his minuscule refrigerator.

"He's taking in the slack on a lot of bad luck." DeFord sat on one of the twelve window seats that tipped great tables of light onto the loft floor. He had discovered scrap leather in an old barrel and was whittling a dog collar as Leggatt paced under the skylight, lifting sheeting from paintings. "Why do you keep your pictures covered?"

"I tend to remember them as better than they are and become resigned to their weaknesses," Codgers said, measuring a paste of yogurt, chili powder, turmeric, fenugreek, coriander and cumin. "So I cover them and surprise myself. The experience of the canvas atop my compromised memory is often very helpful. And always somewhat discouraging . . . What will you do with those leather strips?"

"I'll soak seven in water, then braid them around a dry one. Do you ever think you have been too easily—satisfied with recognizing evil—and so you have not gone on?"

"Ha!" Codgers' hairless face swiveled. "And where might you suggest I go, Mr. DeFord?"

"He nearly had you for a moment there," Leggatt said.

"Yes," Codgers squeaked. "Perhaps he still does. People experience their opinions very early. Then reason appears, truths are illuminated. But opinions remain. Yes, I may be lying to myself. I'm a limited man, and when I

was younger I learned badly and saw mostly with my eyes. My pain tolerance was low. And so I lied. I learned too little. Now it has become much more difficult to convince myself I can learn at all. So I may be obliged to lie."

"But you paint beautifully."

"Thank you, Mr. DeFord. But your belief in me does not make it true. I may be lying without knowing."

"And if they are beautiful lies."

"Then it is art."

Leggatt had uncovered a half dozen paintings and was studying them over the edge of his coffee cup. "Goddamn —I'd almost forgotten this sort of thing could be done."

"You sound tired," Codgers squeaked. "You've over-extended yourself."

"You seem petulant. You've underestimated yourself. You advised a half dozen entanglements for me. 'You're worthy of it.' Acknowledging your advice is costing me a hell of a lot of sleep."

"You never sleep." Codgers wrinkled his button nose. "Four, five hours a night, I would guess. Always at war —civil and foreign. You are too young yet—you never sleep."

"Regrets?"

"Of course. But none that matter. Were I to be at war again, never to allow myself to sleep . . . a surgeon, I'd be a surgeon."

"And your painting?" asked DeFord.

"I paint perfectly now. But that is not enough. Not since the Greeks has it been enough. I started too late." Codgers examined his parchment hands. "I'd be a surgeon next time and paint too late again, I don't doubt. Oh yes, I'd like a dozen lifetimes. Then a dozen more. Man is cheated, Mr. DeFord. Cheated short."

"Perhaps you cheat yourself thinking so."

"Johnie, is it your third Bowery anniversary we are

supposed to be ignoring by this dinner or your third birthday?"

"Both."

"Apparently . . . Fear, Mr. DeFord, I talk of fear. I would submit each man organizes himself in terms of that which he fears. As a child I recognized the eternal unequal possession of wealth. So I became a banker to affect that to which I feared I might fall victim. And the more effective my banking, the more I found the inequality of distribution. I became expert in distribution, and in the process, effected it quite favorably in my direction. It was becoming one with the rich that lent me my first insight. Nothing at all new—one of those perceptions constantly being imbued with all sorts of sentimental tragedy. I discovered the rich were stupid. They possessed nothing. Is it surprising such a pathetic and minuscule insight would take so long? No matter. But fear, you see, fear was still affecting. I then became a teacher, satisfied my discovery of fear was enough. Sufficiently egotistical to believe one had to be, one had to give oneself in service. Trying to balance out a lifetime of accumulation by a lifetime of distribution. Fear."

"And now you are free."

"Of fear, Mr. DeFord? I have individual enemies: a loose carpet, an unnoticed draft. But fear? No."

"A marvelous escape."

"Your obsession with escape is very poetical, Johnie. But for me utterly worthless. You are the kind who cannot live in a rabbit warren, are driven suicidal by public media, are incapable of respecting the populace, the herd. Not that you should. When the populace behaves unpredictably and individually, they will be respected. Until that time they must respect themselves in lieu or in ignorance of being respected by those who no longer operate out of fear. But it is death for you to live with them—and so your affair with escape, I would rather say exile. You are native exile. Myself? I could live anywhere. And do."

Codgers turned up the flame under his onions, added curry paste and danced at the sizzling pan, constantly scraping the paste free of the hot metal. "Yogurt!" Leggatt leaped to cool the mixture. "Not too much! It took me twenty-six years to learn this properly." Leggatt stood with readied spoon while Codgers scraped and the yogurt disappeared. "Yogurt!"

Leggatt spooned. "How long do you keep this up?"

"You . . . have to . . . fuse the curry with onions"—the spatula rotated furiously—"smell the flavor. Secret is: can't let it burn . . . Yogurt!"

Leggatt spooned. "What will you get this time?"

"Idiot! Ten spices, five possible yogurts, four basic ingredients, half dozen garnishes, side dishes, etcetera—and you ask specifics. I'm trying for the one we had last month. Once more with the yogurt, Johnie." Codgers lowered the flame, sank into a chair and folded his hands, watching the simmering mixture with a dreamy stare. "There's garbanzo juice in the icebox. Add exactly a half cup, and we'll let it cook."

"It's like a goddamn doll's house in this corner."

Codgers pouted. "I lived in a trailer once. Became accustomed to all kitchen things in one place."

On the street below, a fire-engine pumper burst red and clanging from its brick house, firemen jerking at their boots. The hook-and-ladder piece jackknifed after it, tail steerer almost directly under DeFord, madly cranking his wheel as if it were connected to the wailing sirens. But DeFord barely noticed, for on the sidewalk Joe Raven stood watching until all sound and glitter faded. Then Raven deliberately looked up and grinned. DeFord stepped back, for the second time that day passing his hand over his face as if to wipe something from it. Codgers saw the gesture and stepped silently to the window. When he turned, his face was bland and innocent.

"There was a time, Mr. DeFord, when the traditional hero made peace with his friends and killed his enemies."

"Golden days." Leggatt returned to sipping coffee in front of the paintings.

"It was the way a man defined himself, you might say. Now men are all trying to make peace with their enemies and outproduce their friends."

"He would call that sort of rationalization wisdom."

"It is neither. Rationalization is finding bad reasons for what you believe on instinct—which is just as much instinct." The old man seized DeFord's arm and made a face at Leggatt's back. "And wisdom, Johnie, wisdom is the ability to withdraw successfully from a bad game." When Leggatt did not turn, Codgers prodded DeFord again. "I am no longer a hero. I cannot risk myself again in the game. But you are, Johnie. You should fall in love."

"I am always falling out of love."

"You dramatize everything. I mean a woman."

Leggatt turned. "What? Again? Once again?"

Codgers pranced to his stove and hid his face in steam. "Don't be naïve, Johnie. You are a different man than even a month ago. A man like you is a different man from woman to woman. That's why they never work for you. They teach you something about yourself, you become a different person, and the new Johnie falls out of love. You are what is called in some circles, a late bloomer. Try again."

"Were you ever married, Mr. Codgers?"

"I have been married on six different occasions, Mr. DeFord. And never to the same woman. And I have eighteen children."

Leggatt's eyes narrowed. "Where?"

"I have absolutely no idea. From time to time half of them left me, and I left the other half."

"How the hell can you stand there stirring your brew and recommend such a thing for me?"

"Because . . . because you deserve it, Johnie. You're worthy of it."

"It would be a lot of living," Leggatt said softly.

"Not for you, Johnie."

"Don't you ever . . . ?" DeFord bent over the sink, stretching his wet leather.

"Get lonely, Mr. DeFord? Yes. Sometimes. I could visit my children, they are all successful; one reason I live here. I provided for them so well I have little money left. But I don't visit my children, as they are too dull. Old men and crotchety old women, my children." He poured rice, measuring its level with his finger and adding water to the second joint.

"Character." Leggatt carefully moved a painting out of the sun to study it. "Character. Character."

Codgers tiptoed to the sink and whispered to DeFord, "When I first knew Johnie his ideas were like elephants trying to stand on their heads." He called aloud, "You have character, Johnie."

"Character? Jesus Christ. Character is what others see, characteristics exist for others. When I examine them for myself, they crumble. Fuck character! I should stand here performing so people can sense me as character. 'He is a memorable character.' Or 'Mr. Leggatt has created a truly remarkable character of himself for our time.' Yes, yes," Leggatt muttered, "character. Give them a little action, Johnie, keep the old life moving along."

"By the way, your brother—"

Leggatt turned. "Has Frank been visiting again?"

"Of course. I made my fried breakfast salad. For lunch —it's too much for me in the mornings now. He came to ask after you; one of his friends bought your canvas of the park, Johnie. Two hundred and fifty."

"Well. I never thought . . . well, damn. We're rich, DeFord! Where's the check?"

"Franklin said it had been made over to him, so he wanted to give you cash."

As if it were made of ash, Leggatt carefully put his cup down, and staring into it, slipped his hands out of sight in his rear pockets. "That makes five of the damn things Frank's hidden in his attic."

The old man squeaked on as if he had not heard. "He was very anxious to see you. And very charming."

"Frank's in love with money; it brings out all his charm. But he's buried me under his ideas of me, and the poor devil doesn't know who he's trying to help: the me he's lost or the me he's created."

Codgers leaned over the sink to watch DeFord weave his leather. "And if you could have him accept you, understand you? If he would want to change his life because of you?"

Leggatt examined his hands. "All right. I would think I was shallow, even that I was wrong. What have you two got there?"

"Interesting. I've seen men plait three, five, or seven and nine. But eight strands, Johnie—you don't see that any more. Old cattlemen braided their lariats in an eight-strand weave, didn't they, Mr. DeFord?"

"For close-in work. That was a long time ago, when rope wouldn't hold its stiffness long less it was soaked. And then it lost strength." His hands crimped and kneaded. "I learned it forty-seven years ago in Colorado. From a man who remembered. Would you like a turn?"

The old man's face wrinkled upwards as his hands jumped. "Ah! This strand goes here, yes? . . . Forty years ago I had retired and was touring this country—this goes here, I see—but even then I did not find anyone who could do this. No, I have it wrong, over here. Ah, I have lost the leader. You'd best take it back, Mr. DeFord. I cannot keep it snug. Yes, you try, Johnie . . . Ah, you're good with it."

Leggatt straightened. "No. I can hold it tight, but I can't follow the pattern. How will you fasten it?"

"I'll measure the dog's neck, then braid it loose enough to slip if he gets caught on anything. Then I think I'll rest."

"Ready in two hours; we'll wake you." Codgers stirred the seared chicken and its broth into his curry. "And now, Johnie, what's in your pack?"

"Divorces. Broken marriages. Misalliances between hand and eye. But there's two I especially want you to see."

"Ah!" said Codgers. "Now these two . . . yes. Yes. Your line, Johnie, your intellection. It imposes upon the color. And you push it. To the edge. The way you are living, is it not? A roll above the river. Ah, but the painting of it! Your lines grow from the canvas; your color is breathed upon them. Yes, it is perfectly painted. Perfectly. But how you cleave to judgments, statements. You won't make much of a living—people seek other forms for that. Yes, you'll have to wait until the new experiments exhaust themselves. Already they place a man's studio for sale as a work, a work, mind you—where must we go from there? Back to the intellect of line, the feel of color. To what you have here—the responsible, the thoughtful. Here, on this one—see?"

"But?"

"But?"

"There is always a 'but.' "

"Only if you insist. Your painting is full of greatness. It simply hasn't collected itself. It doesn't shout. Oh no. You and a few others. Your time will come. We must go back to the canvas, you know. Some of us, at least. Soon the greatness will be known."

"In the meantime, I must feed myself."

"Don't be ridiculous. Your friends will feed you. What are friends for?"

When DeFord measured, the dog shivered badly but calmed to his voice: "If you're to stay with me you'll need a collar." Without expression Sheriff watched him walk to the far corner, where he lay on a cot to finish the braiding. DeFord worked slowly and meticulously, while Leggatt talked with Codgers beyond rows of sculpture and paintings in a labyrinth of bookcases that seemed to advance like pickets from the nook where the old man cooked, slept and worked. Cases of leatherbacked books and portfolios were well sanded and polished—good work, DeFord judged. Yet the majority were unfinished and held worn paperbound books, as if Codgers had finally run out of time. It saddened DeFord to guess Codgers' age; extremely old people saddened him. They survived both change and failure, outlived contemporaries and family and senility and death, held out until, by tenacity or strength or luck, they had clung to twenty or even thirty years of great age. A person so old would be beyond worrying his heart or lungs. It was great lasting, great luck, but it saddened him nonetheless—as an old carnival elephant had once, when he was a boy. Standing gray in the sun, so impossibly wrinkled. Standing as if forgotten. No, he thought, it is just that I am tired. Lately I think this way when tired. With his hands he stretched the collar firm, then lay back and closed his eyes, hearing Sheriff pad over to him and the satisfied grunt when the dog curled under the cot. Then he passed into such a dreamless sleep it seemed only a moment before Leggatt touched his shoulder.

Codgers' elaborate curry lay beyond the maze of bookcases, completely covering a table with its platters and bowls. DeFord's impulse was to shy away, but if he approached it not as supper or dinner but as a hot barbecue—a complex of Mexican chili—then he could eat almost as well as Leggatt, who seemed bottomless. The tastes were confusing; he lost the locations of textures and heat, so each helping was another surprise. Yet most pleasing was that neither Codgers nor Leggatt said anything: DeFord thought of wordy explanations as impositions. He had not put so many things between his teeth that he could not learn something different, but he distrusted wrapping new experiences in a plexus of words. It was trying to talk them good. When he emptied his last helping, Codgers said, "I hope you've enjoyed yourself," and offered a mug of steaming black coffee so perfectly anticipating his appetite, he felt both grateful and awkward. But the old man seemed to anticipate that as well, and without waiting for an answer, pointed beneath the sink. "I have been feeding your dog—hope you do not object. Amazing animal—he's eaten a good bit of everything."

Leggatt scraped the bottom of each bowl as he carried it to the sink. "I knew two old sailors on Elizabeth Street who preferred antifreeze to Scotch. This is an Elizabeth Street dog, isn't it?"

"With a preference for *dalhbat, chapati* and Greek olives. But now with a collar of his own, an Elizabeth Street dog in address only."

"A dog clever enough to know fine cooking is next to none, but a dog that can cook it," DeFord said. "And with you around, Johnie, he'd have to. To get a bite in edgewise."

"It's not Johnie's fault, Mr. DeFord. After all, he's providing for his cause as well."

"Cause?"

"Himself. In Johnie you see a man who secretly resents being born; he'd rather have plunked himself into existence."

"By his own hair."

"Exactly."

Leggatt strolled to a window and lit a cigarette while he looked up and down the sidewalk. "So it will be an even match, I'll wait until you're both a little sharper before I take you on." He stood whistling to himself and smoking while Codgers pranced in his corner, lowering dishes into soapy water. "It's almost six now. I'll go back and pick up the shirt, then pass by here and—"

"No." DeFord stood. "It's my job, so I'll go along with you."

When they were halfway down the stairs Codgers called from above, where he stood drying his small parchment-colored hands. "Elephants, Mr. DeFord. Like elephants trying to stand on their heads."

VII

The pear-shaped man squatted in the One Miler, staring vacantly across his table at a man resting face down, hands over head as if to cushion a beating. This time DeFord made no effort to be alone while Leggatt negotiated with Bert. Whether because of Codgers' banquet or his anticipation of the walk across the island city, or simply that the bar was warm with movement—whatever, DeFord felt less compromised. When you feel you can fill a doorway, you owe it to yourself to fill one, he thought, deliberately taking a seat at Pearshape's table. When he stretched his legs aside for Sheriff, Pearshape's eyes struggled and his tic jumped.

"You. Want to talk with me, you?" Pearshape swam free of his dream, face pumping. "Listen. You got troubles, I don't want to know nothing." DeFord stared, never allowing the spaniel eyes to escape. "But fifty bucks . . .

and you won't have to move. I'll have the package brought right here. What. You say? . . . I didn't think so."

"I don't want your money."

"Sure. You want Bert's money. You want to take Eddie's shirt and chinky-chinky-Chinaman it crosstown. Know you. Know all about you." Pearshape carefully collected himself in his chair, becoming a very powerful fat man. "Failure. Easiest thing in the world to achieve. Greater losers, lesser losers—know my money's no different from Bert's. But not you. You're something special. An old loser. A borrowed loser, a blue loser. Bullshit." He reached to the third man collapsed at their table. "Like your buddy here. He's something special too, he thinks."

"That you, DeFord?" Tanner lifted his head and tried a smile. "I'm all . . . fucked up, neighbor." Bert's laughter burst over Tanner's swollen face, rooting DeFord to his chair.

"You. Don't worry your wino lawyer friend. He'll swill himself sober again. Then talk himself drunk."

DeFord watched Bert pull himself from Leggatt and drag his damp rag along the bar toward Tanner, who finger-combed his hair and drew himself erect. "A drink? A drink? What you think I'm on Bowery for? The air?" Tanner sipped wine and leaned elbows on the wood.

"Further reason you can't turn that damn clock back just anytime you choose, Bert. Question of public or private domain."

"Give me something that works," Remember called.

"Don't interrupt. It's this simple, Bert: your bucket is no longer private domain, because it maintains too vital a service. People don't come here as to other bars. They come as to a hospital, church, that kind of trash."

Bert lowered his glass and exposed gat teeth. "You mean I no longer own this place?"

"Not exactly. Think of it this way: a man is responsible for the sidewalk portion of his real property. Maintenance, safety, that kind of stuff; but he can't close it off, it's public domain whether—"

"You"—Pearshape had slumped again to his fat man's disguise and offered DeFord his secret fat man's wink—"want Bert's money. Your friend Johnie needs money. Get it from his brother Frank. You get yours from Bert. Bert gets his from Tanner, the rest of these losers—"

"What the hell, Tanner"—Bert motioned Leggatt to wait—"you on some sort of civil rights wagon?"

"I am not on any wagon. Point of fact: none of my best friends are. Second thought: maybe one." He twirled his tumbler, toasting DeFord in a gesture for understanding.

Studiously Bert slid a full glass to him. Just as gently, he asked, "Trial? Huh? You'll hire another jury?"

"How'd I come out last week?"

"Against capital punishment. Jury split."

"It must have cost you plenty."

"Fifth apiece." Tanner studied his billfold. After a while he pushed his money across the wood, and Bert pocketed the bills and poured.

"I know. Been asking around. Listen, Tall Man. Listen, Special Loser. It goes nice, tight. This guy Frank Leggatt buys out Bert—a year later Bert ends up here."

DeFord watched Tanner's jury shuffle into the light as Bert's apron swooped through the bull pen, leaving a dribble of laughter and a trail of disappointed faces. He saw Leggatt signal Bert, trying to contract the job with the shirt, but the bar crowded up, the jury sat and Tanner stood alone with a pitcher of wine.

"My name is Jaxon Tanner, and by city ordinance nine-two-seven-three, I am licensed to practice law in this borough." Punctuating with sips, swallowing tumblers at a pause, Tanner paced, gestured, cajoled, reasoned, insinuated and threatened while behind him stood the bartender-judge, tongue tip wriggling his gat teeth.

DeFord watched his face purple with wine and effort while his jury nodded, drinking less as Tanner sentence by sentence virtually hauled each man straight on his stool. He felt the crowd press close to enjoy; he saw Tanner again toast his health in a gesture for understanding.

"The clocks have to be set for standard time soon, and I say Bert shouldn't set them back for his sleeping time in the morning, but should set them back for your drinking time in the evening."

"Your friend Tanner comes down here for Frank Leggatt. Get some last papers signed. Bert wines him off his wagon. Meets that crazy Indian. Bert keeps him wino for a year. Raven cleans him out." He ceased talking when Leggatt came through the crowd.

"You want to wait down the street with some coffee?" Leggatt asked.

"I'll stay." By now DeFord was sure the job with Eddie's shirt had failed, but there seemed nothing to do but wait till Leggatt realized it.

"Proudhomme was by a moment ago. Wanted you to talk with Raven. But when we get the shirt we'll duck out the back."

"We're not going to get the shirt, and you know it."

Leggatt leaned over the table. "I don't understand you. Bert has Eddie's shirt under his bar. Cleaned and packaged. Waiting for what? Who knows? A whim. A change of mood. Waiting till he gets bored with beating Jaxon again and turns charitable. Waiting for anything. But he won't even speak to me now. I thought you understood it would be like this from the beginning."

DeFord spoke slowly, as if instructing a child. "It's not the way it should be."

"Should be! Nothing's the way it should be! Make one

too many mistakes—stop eating your own dream—lose something you take for granted—you'll wake up on Elizabeth Street. Then things will be the way they should—" Leggatt's eyes softened. "You old bastard, what makes you come onto me like you'd gentle a horse?"

"Who taught you of gentling horses?"

"Women." Leggatt stood back. "Well, I'll play with Bert and steal pretzels for Sheriff. Where is he, waiting outside?"

"No, he's—"

"Probably in the back. I'll find him."

DeFord did not hear. He was staring between his feet, where Sheriff had been, his heart beating hollowly as the fear Leggatt had brought thumped away. Naked. Naked.

"So before I turn to precedent, I'll admit it's difficult to decide whether private property, after long and continuous public use, becomes more public domain and less private domain. And all that trash."

No, Sheriff was not in the bar, DeFord was certain now. No one was bending to stroke or tease or tempt, no one paid mind but to Tanner. And Pearshape kept talking. What in the name of God did the man want?

"Leggatt's brother Frank. Bert. Raven. Tanner . . ." Pearshape eased his stale wine at DeFord. "Eleven cents' profit in that glass, Tall Man. And you mean to say you don't want my money? Think my package is dirtier than Bert's ex - partner - now - Frank - Leggatt's - partner Eddie's fucking chinky-Chinaman-cleaned shirt?"

"That's my affair." DeFord stared the white face back into its dream and pushed to the bar. But by the time Bert shuffled to him, he realized Leggatt had gone.

"Shirt? Oh yeah. Like I told Johnie, I'm not sure I want it to go over to Eddie tonight"—his tongue moved with the slick of the bar rag—"but I don't see how it would make much difference to Johnie. He ducked out. Yeah.

That little faggot of Raven's came back with some sort of leather collar. Johnie didn't say nothing. Just followed him on out." He showed his teeth. "Guess they got a date, huh, pops?"

◇ ◇ ◇

His crushed legs beneath him, Joe Raven squatted on dry brick rubble, stirring hot coals with a charred stick-ball bat as he scattered dry sand from a rusty can to smother the flames threatening to burn the pieces of broiling meat. And he said, "I-have some pid-gin too, Johnnie, if you'd be hungry for-that." Each word came by itself through a bemused and dreamy smile as if language were an alien ritual, vaguely amusing.

Leggatt stood on the other side of the fire, eyes turned from the flames. "What do you want to talk about?"

"Talk-about? I don't want to talk-about any-thing, Johnie. I wanted to in-vite the old-man to visit." Raven's hand passed under his sleeve; the shining drill of his ice pick probed the dark meat, then reversed its arc, and his hand hung empty. "I'm disappointed. The old-man's dog came to visit. That-right, Crook?"

"And stayed, Joe. And stayed for dinner." Crook's laugh was a silent bubbling, ending in a choked grunt when he pushed up with his knuckles and advanced on the fire to cut a piece of the half-cooked meat. Knees slightly bent, he swung away, catching Proudhomme and lifting him from the scaly rubble as he jabbed the meat at his face. "Try a piece, Alfred."

"Take it away! Joe! Oh, Joe! Joe!"

Raven smiled but continued to spread sand over DeFord's pension check until everything was obliterated but its signature block. Then he said, "That's enough, Crook," and Crook let Proudhomme slip away. Again Raven's hand passed under his sleeve, but this time darted at the edge of the fire to skewer a breast of pigeon. Without looking up from the coals, he held his ice pick to Proudhomme, who circled around Crook, plucked the pigeon and nibbled. After a while Raven lifted his face. "Are-n't you par-tic-ular, Alfred? Are-n't you?"

Proudhomme averted his face from the darker meat, extending a limp hand when Raven offered a bottle. But Raven's pick carved the dusk where the bottle shone dull red. As the glinting drill etched its figure eight, Proudhomme's hand kept reaching to the bottle, then flipping away. Raven teased awhile. "Being par-tic-ular, Alfred, you should have white-wine with your-bird. But I for-got and bought port for our first little-guest."

Crook filled his mouth. "He stayed for dinner Joe, didn't he?"

Raven's pick vanished and he held the bottle to Proudhomme. "Poor Al-fred. Haven't had a-drink all afternoon, have-you? Finish it."

"It's our last bottle, Joe."

"It's Al-fred's now. Here, take-it." He rocked on his haunches, smiling as Proudhomme drank. With the smile still there, he looked up at Leggatt. "I want-this check signed!"

"If you give it to me, DeFord will sign it." Leggatt watched Raven's half-closed eyelids, almost translucent in the dry heat of the fire.

"I know he-will sign-it. But if he does-n't bring it back"—the lids slid open on black pupils iridescent in their brownish whites—"bring it to me him-self . . ."

Leggatt squatted. "Why DeFord, Joe? What do you hold against DeFord?"

"Crook? Shall I tell-him, Crook?" Raven pitched dried weeds on the embers, and in their rattling light Leggatt saw a heavy shadow move behind him. Then he was tipped backwards, grasped so he could not breathe as Raven leaped through the fire to land on his waist.

"Bitch! Bitch! You got him, Joe!"

"Shut-up, Alfred." Proudhomme stopped his dancing. "Let him up a-bit so he can see." Slowly Raven lifted Leggatt's shirt and pressed the ice pick against his bare stomach. His shoulder rolled as if to punch it in, but stopped. "How do-you feel now, John-nie?"

"Alive . . . alive."

The ice pick went away.

The long arms dropped from behind Leggatt, and Crook retreated, still ready to spring out of the firelight. Leggatt tried to stand but his knees collapsed, so he sat, breathing hard. Raven was back at his bed of coals, the weeds burned to nothing, leaving a deep blackness encircled by a skeleton of white ash.

"Joe—for crissake—"

"He-runs. That's why. That old-man runs. He runs."

"May I go now?"

For a long while Raven said nothing. Then he looked up. "You send him back-with his check. Now reach-over and take-it."

"Hand it to me."

"No, John-nie."

Leggatt stretched over the coals, trying not to breathe the rich meat odor. But Raven snatched his wrist downwards until the heat burned at his stomach.

"Yes. Alive . . . all the way-down as I fell. I was-alive. Never so-alive as then."

◇ ◇ ◇

Holding his coat tight to his stomach, Leggatt picked his way over the crushed brick, starting visibly when DeFord rose from the shadows. "I guess he didn't have time to slip loose." Leggatt passed him the pension check and held out Sheriff's collar. "Come on, we've got to get to your place fast. Pack you up so you can spend the night at Codgers' loft."

DeFord did not hear. The pain has come in a different place, he was thinking. Strange. When he saw the black-and-tan killed, he barely guessed how it would be to lose Sheriff. But it was not at all as he imagined. Now he was filled with nothing but numbness, a numbness souring to a sullen and angry insistence to keep on with everything: the shirt, Tanner, the return to Oregon. Commitments now, much more than want or need—they were contracts. Causes. And enveloping his angry determination to tough them through was his wonder at the pain. I shall have to relearn pain. The admission dizzied him.

"This way. We'll get you packed—"

"No. No, no. No . . . the job may be lost, but I promised Tanner I'd see him home. So at least I'll do that."

Leggatt shook his head, laughed, and as if startled by the explosion of his own voice, hid his hands and was silent. But as they crossed toward the One Miler he laughed again. "I think you weren't close enough to that fire. But then, perhaps I was too close. Can you be too close? Joe has a message, all right." He touched his stomach gently. "Alive." They walked together, moving nervously but in step through the aimless drift of Saturday night on Bowery. "Alive. Alive."

◇ ◇ ◇

"So you ask, what's the difference? Well, what is the difference?" Tanner's hands explored his swollen face. "Oh Jesus," he whispered, "does it really make any difference whether I sit in here and get drunk or go out and get elected mayor of New York?" He smiled and whispered to his wine, "Balance is all." The jury was mute.

Tanner looked from man to man. Then he put down his glass. "I rest my case." Wineless, Tanner stepped carefully from Bert's bar and moved toward DeFord. "That you, neighbor? You said you'd come back, didn't you? Listen, I got to tell you something—"

"All right! Let's cast the ballots. Do I turn the clock back on your time or on mine?" The judge set out pitchers and his jury shuffled, but Tanner turned his back to them all and came to DeFord.

"I'll take you home now. Can you walk alone?"

"Walk, DeFord? Some. Some. Vision down to a tunnel, though"—he made a loop with thumb and forefinger—"thirty caliber. You know, inside it's tunnel vision too." Tanner finger-combed his hair and bulged his eyes at DeFord. "And it says, 'Get out of Elizabeth Street, DeFord. Let Raven have your check and get out. Pack up. Go.'" Tanner seemed rooted, sightless, to the floor.

DeFord supported him, and with Leggatt helping, they had little trouble until Bert stopped them. "I thought you guys'd never come back. Just tallied the ballots. Old Tanner lost again"—he pushed Eddie's shirt over the bar—"so everybody wins tonight."

"You are a son of a bitch, Bert. Right to the bottom."

"Ah, Johnie."

"No matter," said DeFord. "We don't want your money."

Leggatt touched him. "We don't?"

"No." I have been wrong all day about this, he realized. Tanner I can help. And give Johnie a hand finding his brother, now we have my check. But check or no, I can't take this money. Broke or no, I'd eat out of garbage cans first and learn to climb to the bottom of Johnie's ladder to sleep. "No."

"No." Leggatt pursed his lips. "No . . . okay, easy come, easy go. Shove your fucking shirt, Bert."

"Wait. When I win, it's free drinks. One thing you got to say: I run a friendly bar." He hurried two tumblers on the wood.

"Shove them too." They moved Tanner again.

"Bert? Give me something that works."

"A minute, Remember. Listen, you guys. Wait. Admit I run a friendly bar, huh?"

"All right. You run a friendly bar."

"Something that works!"

Tanner squinted to focus on Remember. "Try some river water, neighbor."

"Tell your lush friend I'll find something before that, all right."

"For crissake, shut up! Listen, Johnie, to show you just what a friendly place I run here, these drinks'll be waiting for you. Now what more you want, huh . . . ? Huh?"

◇ ◇ ◇

The gun-blue sky was all stars, trapping the two combines that ate their way back and forth and the four trucks they fed at the end of each mile run. In the combine lights, the wheat riffled and streaked as if tipped by the wings of some hunting night bird, miles of golden wheat heads dissolving in front of the thin prow of the lamps while the huge machine lifted and rolled with the prairie swell, its engine at a steady howl, wheat incessantly pouring into its grain bin.

By the second night, the lay of the field and its attending trucks had become so unreal yet so predictable it all seemed to DeFord not so much an endless punishment but that sort of impossible test a man faces once in his life. A thing a man attacks out of rage, exhaustion, and pain, to finally surmount not by any of these but by the sort of brute endurance that in the end has little resemblance to anger or even rage: a mindless endurance that does not even seem to belong to the man himself. Yet at the end of each run, when he was forced to brake the wheels of his machine—its engine never stopped—forced to punch the lever that poured fifty bushels into the truck, then his very movement brought the field to its proper dimensions: one mile wide by five miles long. The first day he climbed down to stretch while they gassed, but later he did not. The ground ladder was ten feet long with nine steel rungs. And going into the second day, he knew that once he swung over the side his legs would not work to bring him back.

The beginning was clear. It was Kansas in 1952 or—his mind slipped—was it the year later? No matter. With a builder of grain bins he had driven east from California for the biggest money job he ever held: supervising construction of the wood frames that supported the great steel drums.

It was the days on the machine he could barely remember. Yet if he began with meeting the combiners and their boss—a short, muscled man who squatted on his heels to talk while his crew waited for the morning dew to evaporate—if he thought of that he could remember the time clearly. Eight A.M. of a Friday.

He forgot what had happened to the first combine man, lost that memory somewhere in the field the first night. An accident, he guessed. Someone was needed—the truckers were Mexican boys, nice boys, but no hand with machinery. So he took the job, and abruptly things went against them. The third combine slid on a terrace and overturned; the fourth threw its feed belt; the fifth's hydraulics kept bleeding out until it stood useless in the center of miles of wheat, its header scoop pointed skywards like some paleolithic monster lowering at the cumulonimbus that threatened hail or rain. The wheat would not wait. Each head had cured, its beard brittle as glass slivers; all thousand acres had broiled to death under the sun, the yellowed heads a lake of mirrors, each reflecting to each and to the ground itself until the stalks were the color of hammered and rolled gold. The team of them paused at the edge of this impossibility left with their two insignificant machines, wondering what would come first: hail to beat it all into cattle bedding or the dew to prohibit its storage. With the trucks waiting at either end, DeFord and the owner's son began. All that first day the clouds slowed and layered but moved on under a hard flat sun. When the evening dewpoint stayed down, he kept on—at first a joke, a game between himself and the owner's boy, then something else, which both men respected and said nothing about.

And none of them knew his name: that was the first distortion. That after eighteen hours he was still nameless struck him so suddenly he laughed aloud. But the sound frightened him, and all through the night he guarded himself lest anything grow out of the miles of grain wallowing under his lights. For images were always just ahead: faces, animals, things. And he knew that if he paid them mind, he would have to stop for them.

About sunrise the boy fell asleep, went through a fence and down into a storm ditch, where the feeder belt dutifully carried a half bushel of rocks into the thrasher housing before it jammed on a handful of broken sickle teeth. So DeFord kept on while the others swapped parts into one of the rigs that had gone gunnysack the day before: vulturing through a pile of links and twisted metal at the edge of that sea of wheat.

The second distortion concerned the grain itself: that it would lie rotting, attacked by rodents, insects, a dozen other blights, costing more in storage than its flour could ever bring. DeFord had heard enough over the café tables to know the price of wheat in a thirty-cent bread loaf.

Two cents. The other twenty-eight were called by wheat men "boondoggle." At the crest of exhaustion the suggestion of those thousand gleaming elevators stuffed with millions of gradually rotting bushels could nearly deceive him. But always he remembered the issue was not boondoggle, or even wheat itself. The issue was threshing before the hail. The issue was making another mile to the north truck, swinging back with an even cut and making another mile to the south truck.

The last distortion was the money: after years of building houses, it was consulting for the shiny food tombs that would be the single thing to round out his stake to a house of his own. This was troubling him greatly when, during the afternoon of the second day, all the distortions were finally eclipsed by the nameless thing that possessed him until the very last cut, the absurd worm of dust, the insect-choked triumphant horn.

He was paid off in Routon, Kansas—a crossroads, not a town—and two days later the money was still in his wallet, carried out and back over the huge field on his hip. Sitting on two thousand dollars for fifty hours, until the boss finally called him down when the generator brushes went, and lying in the stubble, unable to move or walk, he was told the job was done. The field was so large they had not known themselves, but an absurdly turbulent worm of dust had crawled up the dirt road, growing into a speeding pickup whose horn signaled the last cut had been made along the south fence. The words had eased him free enough from his exhaustion to feel his wallet embedded like a rock in his ham. And he was trying to throw it away when he saw the money. It meant nothing. A thin wedge of colored paper an infant might collect pressed into a ridiculous and elaborate fold of leather. He was staring as if it were something washed up at his feet from another shore when the outfit boss gently took it away and helped him to the pickup. In the hotel the combine team undressed him, laid him down, and twelve hours later when he woke, they had already followed the sun northeast into Nebraska. The wallet was in the hotel safe, thicker by fifty dollars. That was the end of it.

◇ ◇ ◇

On the corner of Elizabeth and Prince, Tanner went down on one knee, and his full weight dragged DeFord from his memory. Leggatt, who had been guiding at Tanner's left, stood for a long moment before slowly taking his arm. Once again Tanner's legs began their rubbery march. "Sorry, boys."

"My fault."

Leggatt sounded tired, but DeFord had come into his second wind with the memory of Kansas. Except for his heart, wasn't he the same man but ten years older who had lasted fifty hours, until a machine, not he, burned a piece of itself out? Only his heart had changed, and perhaps it had forgotten, for when he listened it seemed to be doing quite well. The prospect of moving from his Elizabeth Street room was cheering, and although he could not afford much better, perhaps the doctors would let him go home soon. Even if he must wait an entire month, he would get back before the slopes of vine maple lost their bronze and flame and while the timber-line peaks were fresh with snow. Perhaps Codgers would—no, he discarded the idea of living with Codgers; the entire loft was hardly room for the old man himself. But I could visit, at least.

As they turned into his building Tanner stumbled, and again Leggatt was not quick enough. Yes, Johnie is tired, DeFord thought; on his feet since sunup, where I've already long rested at the loft.

But Tanner did so much better navigating the stairs

that Leggatt perked up. "He must have a pint under his mattress."

"What you say, Sergeant?"

"Nothing, nothing."

Tanner's room was exactly DeFord's but one flight closer to the darkened street, with windows so sealed by grime they might have been panes of cement. Tanner fell into his bed and grinned lopsidedly while he inspected the removal of his shoes. "Good work, Sergeant," he said to Leggatt; then to DeFord as his eyelids surrendered altogether: "Thank you, sir."

"I'll go up and pack if you'll wait till he's asleep."

Leggatt had slumped into a chair but looked up, and for a moment his eyes softened. "Anything you say. You seem to have all the rank here." His eyes closed.

DeFord ascended and hurriedly packed, laying Sheriff's collar beside his *Carpenter's Manual,* then quickly closing up the wooden suitcase. If I could take revenge, if there were revenge to take . . . but there was none, had never been. Revenge is all distortion . . . Should I simply walk away? Now that I have my place, should I simply go home to it? As Tanner says . . . ? No. No. Again the renunciation brought a sense of deep strength and shook off his confusion. The issue is to stay with what you start. Returning to Tanner's room, he found Leggatt dead asleep, and so on the remaining scrap of the paper he had lowered to Leggatt that morning, wrote:

> You look played out. Get some rest. Going to store my clothes at Mr. Codgers' place. Swing back for you. We'll find your brother. Get your winter stake.

Then he stepped quickly down into the coolness where the moon was full over the East River, a small worn coin clutched at but always eluding the tenement's grasp. He made Codgers' loft in good time, found the old man about to bed down, his teeth a maniacal grin in a glass of water by the sink. "Here to stay?" Codgers gummed. DeFord shook his head, explained. Codgers nodded. "Come for breakfast. Tell me all about it." DeFord promised and left, whistling, his heart fine now. He was two blocks from Leggatt when Joe Raven stopped him.

Stepping from a dark alleyway beside a partly wrecked building, Raven smiled and passed his hand under his sleeve. The thin gleam of a corner streetlight caught on the long drill of his ice pick, but Raven himself seemed as formless as the shadows clinging to him. He seemed to be waiting for something as DeFord stood his ground, Eddie's shirt under his arm. Although there was no more than ten feet of sidewalk between them, Raven was not looking at DeFord at all. He was looking behind him. In four jumps DeFord was up the stoop, and Proudhomme, who had been inching up, now faced Raven with a two-by-four wobbling in his hands.

Raven laughed without moving his lips. "You-might as-well come down here now, old-man. Or you want we-should get you back into what's there behind-you?"

DeFord stepped backwards into the rotting warren of rooms and hallways, and as Raven started up the stairs he turned and groped into the darkness.

VIII

On a bench in the lobby of the Three Lions, Dee Bee Smith sits lamenting the state of his fingernails. Fingernails will never pass. Busman will know he is not respectable. So what difference even if the rest of disguise works? Of course he could walk. No. He has bought the cheapest pair of respectable shoes he could find, and in a few blocks he would be limping. Besides, he has no socks. You can't buy secondhand socks—even on Bowery. But suit pants hang low and will hide it. That was clever. He spent afternoon spying on Respectables to see what they noticed. They all looked first at a man's color, then his clothes, then whatever he was carrying or doing. But seldom his eyes. Never his socks. Dee Bee smiles at this cunning, but even the slight movement of his face causes his headache to tighten behind his eyes and roar in his ears. Ahhhh. Did he remember to buy a tie? Again he

counts the articles on his fingers, eyes pinching with effort. Yes. That is, he remembers buying a tie. If only he could sneak off to examine disguise again. But he must pretend to watch the blue box. Saturday night he always flops at the Three Lions and watches the blue box. Yes, he must pretend nothing has changed, so he has even gone into wine money in order to watch blue box in order to make Them believe this is a normal Saturday, in order . . . The whole thing makes his brain swell like the hangovers he suffered as a whiskey lush. With his decision for wine he can afford to tie one bottle into the next, and as long as he takes it slowly, hangovers never catch up. Dee Bee moans and lets his hands fall into his lap. It is much too difficult. Fingers will not pass, no matter how much washing.

Dee Bee grins, lets his eyes close and his weary senses crawl toward nothing. But gradually the ache goads him to an old obscenity. The Mucket. He will patent and market the Mucket. A pubic toupee in five different colors, scents, flavors, textures. Be a silky strawberry blonde, a curly coffee-flavored brunette. The pubic toupee —variety, excitement, suspense. Don't fuck it, Mucket.

This does no good; the blue box still bleats. Is it shoes he needs? tie? shirt? clean nails? trimmed hair? His hand retreats to a pocket, where it strokes his piece of silk. But the silk has lost its magic, so pretending thirst he slips outside, and there on the sidewalk of this beloved block Dee Bee Smith is finally soothed.

Careful! Danger! An air-conditioned busload of Them passes slowly. Behind the thick rose-tinted glass their faces float fat and brave. Sightseers. Bowery tour. Lies. Lies. Dee Bee knows. Yes, tomorrow at noon he must walk away to find another block. Whimpering and futilely stroking his silk, he goes back into the Three Lions. To pretend.

Things. Things. Things. Should he be obscene again?

No. It isn't true for him. With his decision for wine, he could leave all obscenity behind. But this posing as a Respectable is like being a lush, a whiskey aristocrat. Tangles and pain and hangovers.

Careful!

"You. You, Smith, you?"

Dee Bee nods once at the pear-shaped man who takes the bench beside him.

"MEMO:
TO: *All branches*
FROM: *Smith, Elizabeth Street*
D. B. Smith wants for nothing."

Holding his hands tight to his chair to keep them from shaking or crawling about in his lap, he waits. Actually, he feels much better now They have sent Their Man. It confirms his suspicions, it demonstrates the wine has been true for him, it proves—

"Sure you don't. Listen, Smith. A guy named Baker told me this is your block. You live here all the time. Now listen, Smith."

Dee Bee nods while Their Man whispers on. Wants a package delivered. Someone will bring it tomorrow morning . . . Yes. Yes. Dee Bee holds his breath, sneaking a look at his right hand. No, hand is not trembling. He nods, holds it out and breathes craftily as Their Man places into it—two fivers!

But Their Man waits, uncertain, the pale triangle of skin under his right eye cocked, trembling, until Dee Bee realizes what he must do. Slowly he returns one of the fivers, wets his lips and struggles: "I'd drink it up. Keep till I give you the pack—pack—kage."

With the aid of a rather formidable tic, Their Man smiles, reaches out to squeeze Dee Bee's shoulder, then seems to think better of it. "You. You're all right, Smith."

Now Pearshape is gone, so Dee Bee strolls past the blue box, out the door, and ambles toward a liquor store. Since Their Man has made contact, They won't be watching any longer tonight, so he is safe. What is good for headache? Port? No, something like sauterne. Yes. Sweet sauterne . . . Ahead, Johnie and the old lumberjack cross onto Elizabeth with Tanner propped between. Just to be on the safe side, Dee Bee flattens into a doorway. But it does not matter. They do not see him.

As he moons along once again, Dee Bee Smith crinkles the fiver in his pocket. "Socks," he whispers. "Socks."

◇ ◇ ◇

Spike, you are coming out. Under DeFord the stair scaffolding teetered as his penknife dug into a heavy upright. All right, I won't rush you. He paused, shifting gently to flex his numbed thighs, and when the pain started again, he returned to his whittling. About an hour, he thought, the blade passing into the wood to its handle. If the tip holds. Even with that, by morning certain—

"I'm getting cold, Joe."

"Poor Al-fred. We need a-fire." Raven hummed a tuneless chant in the darkness below, then addressed himself at the ceiling. "What you-think old-man? Is-it cold up there? If we had-a fire we could sing songs."

"Want a drink," Crook muttered.

"Here, Al-fred." Clinking of small coins. "If we-are to have a fire, we-will need-a bottle to pass a-round."

"Send Crook, Joe. Send Crook. It's dark."

Fire. Faster, he would have to work much faster. The knife dug, caught—too late. Its blade snapped, tip lost in the soft wood. A worm of nausea uncurled in his belly.

"Come over-here, Al-fred." The coins rattled like teeth.

"No, Joe. I—Joe! Let go, stop, Joe! Ow ow owow!"

"Hardly breaking your-skin, Al-fred. Just sharpen-ing its point for-the old-man."

"Ow, Joe! I'll go. I'll go."

"Poor Al-fred. Hurry back-and we will all share a-nice fire."

All right, knife, DeFord thought. You must make bag with a snub nose. He made himself work steadily, rediscovering everything has a design. The knife is designed for eating the beam, the spike designed to hold up the stair frame. There is knife, and spike which is to come free. And there is hand to make knife move. Then there will be brass pipe—his foot touched a section of pipe he had found below, soft enough to bend to a jimmy but stiff enough to lever loose floorboards, which will make a bridge to the roof next door. He worked dumbly, as if the catechism of action alone would save him; the very abracadabracal magic, if worked like beads through his fingers, would free him. Such action, it occurred to him, marked his entire life; he had always set one act upon another, at its chosen time. And he wondered: is it nothing but an exercise—working board by board by board—pass through sixty, seventy years, keeping yourself at something? But is not that better than asking yourself what it is you are making? You have to stop in order to think ahead, and when you stop building houses or grain bins or combining wheat to ask why, will it not all go soft beneath you? In things of wood and nail you could measure your life. As with the habit of your heart. Below, Raven began a tuneless song:

"River winds lift-gulls to high iron
osprey-eagle slide down
put yellow-eyes on the man reaching
until he falls. Slowly to the water
down from windy places
where birds belong."

DeFord ceased working, and the horror quickened over him. He tried to recall Raven's face, tried to will nose, mouth, eyes and cheeks. The presence of Raven was terror, as shapeless as the dark of one's childhood, void of form or habit, without reason, mind or language. It was bottomless horror—the same abyss that threatened when you stopped whatever you were doing and asked questions. It was what lay beneath when you plunged. Faceless, twisted, mindless. If DeFord could not fit Raven into his country, find his place, then his life had been stupid—the plodding of oxen in circles. He whittled anew, never allowing himself to think ahead to pipe, bridge, freedom—only knife and its slow consumption of wood imprisoning spike.

Raven stopped singing. "Crook? Gather kindling so-we can warm up when Al-fred comes-back."

An hour later Leggatt was with him on the shaky flooring, and below, the first of Raven's fires was purring in a handful of shredded wallpaper.

"Got your breath yet?" DeFord whispered.

"Al . . . most."

"Took your time getting here."

"Christ, but I thought it'd take me forever to climb that slatting with Crook grabbing at my feet. Ape nearly got me. Took my time? You're damn lucky I spotted Proudhomme coming back with his bottle and had sense enough to follow. How the hell did you get into such a mess?"

"I figure I've built just a few of these old high-walled places. Guess I just knew where to walk. Figured the stair frame would pry up. Found an old pipe and—"

"How come Raven didn't climb the wall slatting? Or did you figure on that too?"

"Didn't have to. His legs won't do the work. And that big fellow, he tried it, but he's too stout. The little one, he's too shy of it. But you now, I figured if you came along you might just be crazy enough—"

"To run right in the room with them and climb on up with you."

"Something like that."

"Well, just what do you figure on now?"

"A bridge." DeFord tightened their belts around a stack of floorboards. "I just imagine—"

"Don't just imagine anything, damnit. Stay with figuring on."

"You ever see an old leaf spring, Johnie?"

Leggatt sighed. "I just imagine."

"John-nie?" Raven's syllables came from his misshapen body as if he were calling them one by one into existence. "We-are cold and need fire. My friends . . . my-friends need fire need-food only friends I ever-have." Raven stood and swayed. "A-man needs-friends, John-nie. To keep him warm-to share his bottle-to help him a-long and love him. You got-to have love-you got to have some-one who cares. A buddy is what-you need. Someone who under-stands, stays-by and crawls to-you when it-is winter."

"You geeky son of a bitch, what is this?" Leggatt kicked rubble into the stairwell. "Put this on your fires."

"Gentle, Johnie, gentle him," DeFord whispered. "We're shy ten minutes. The window's bound, and I must find more shingling nails to fasten the clamps."

"What the hell do you think I'm giving you? I'm setting him for an hour's show."

"I'll use the-pieces, John-nie. Because I am your buddy. What-ever you kick down-on my head will go-to the fire. I will burn what-ever you give me, John-nie. I will let you kill your-self soon-you wish because I-am your buddy. But we need-you, John-nie. We need another bud-dy. There is Crook here—a good man sometimes says nothing for-three, four days, but then-you give him a pid-gin or a cat and he perks up. There is no-thing he would not do for-you. And Al-fred is a nice boy. I am no good for Al-fred but I love-him. He is my buddy, and we need each-other. Things-have always been so terrible for Al-fred, he suffers for all-of us. Al-fred is too sensitive. He is sensitive for all of-us. That is-why we pick-on him so. But he-knows we tease-him out of love, John-nie. Because we are buddies here on Bow-ry . . ."

Leggatt waved DeFord to his work and kicked more rubbish over the edge. "I need no one. Here. Burn me if you like. If you really want to do me a favor."

Raven picked the studding from the fire. "Oh, John-nie. Don't do it. Let us-talk buddies first. I will give you what you want—but first we-talk. Because may-be this is not what you want. A buddy knows. You want to-die now, but there is more that we could give-you. Need-ding, John-nie. Needing is what we need, we need-you and you-need your buddies. Tell me, John-nie, what other friends you have would be such buddies they-would kill you if that-is what you want? Only with us on Bow-ry we do this. Do any-thing for you. You want to-die? We do this. Be-cause we love you. You want to live? We push away the wood you kick down on us. Be-cause we love you. We-need and you-need."

"Now tell me how I buy in."

"Buy-in? Buy-in? You don't have-to buy-in." Raven sank over his fire, haunches rocking. "I want-ted so many things, John-nie, wanted such wrong-things. It was the wine, John-nie. The badness." His face turned into the red glow, and from each sunken pocket a dribble of tears marked the blades of his cheeks. "Now wine is-gone, John-nie. There is nothing I ask but you come down to-your buddies, where you belong." His arms raised in supplication, his face streaming. "We can-all kick it, John-nie, we can help each-other and love each-other. We are all no-good, John-nie. All no good. But we understand. Johnie?" Raven sank before his fire: silent, small, misshapen, wretched.

DeFord stared until Leggatt stepped hard on the softness of his boot. "Get back to your boards and belts," he whispered. "Get back to work . . . ahh, Joe. What you want me to say, Joe? This man up here is my buddy too. He's exhausted, sleeping under the window. I can't leave him—not until he's rested."

"And he's trusted you with-his check too. You carry it for-him."

Leggatt bowed his head. "Yes."

"John-nie, John-nie. Let-him sleep, then. And you-think it over. No-buddy would push you. We-will wait here, John-nie, we know you need us and we-need you. Think-about it while your friend sleeps. And we will wait-for you."

DeFord worked, leaving Leggatt slumped in a mimicry of resignation. Below, legs snuggled to his chin, Proudhomme stared sentimentally into the shadows where Crook was dozing. Extravagance, DeFord thought. Always a full-rig show handy as bells on a saw. But could Raven be handled otherwise? He did not want to think about it, so he rolled the brass pipe over the shingle nails, binding their belts to the bridging. He worked hard as the nails slid soundlessly in. Should have an iron rolling pin, he thought. Woman's work, while Johnie keeps at his clowning. At the window he jimmied where old paint bound the frame. Six feet across, a cat walked the next roof in the moonlight, while in the alley below something scuttled in broken glass. The cat stopped, then trotted to the shadows. DeFord sighed. It is not your ears I envy, cat, but I'd swap legs with you for the night. The cat reappeared after a bit in the alley below to hunt his quarry in the debris. So the roof door is open, he thought. Good.

"John-nie? What is your buddy doing? He-is doing something with-the window. I can-hear."

"He's rolled in his sleep. He doesn't sleep well any more, Joe. An old man like that." Leggatt spoke loud, and DeFord chanced wrenching the window.

"Crook!" Raven leaped, his face a mask of rage. "Open-your window. Is-that old-man crawling out?"

Crook tore the sash clear of the wall and leered into the moon. "See nothing, Joe."

"Get-a beam. A long-beam from below. If he comes-out knock him down. Like the cats, Crook." Raven fed his fire and grinned at Leggatt. "Crook gets long poles with wire-noose. Snatches cats out-of yards. He likes noosing, John-nie. My buddy Crook will-drag the old-man down like cats he-pulls over the fence while they-hang on for a-while before the noose-strangles. You-tell him, John-nie."

Leggatt buried his face in his hands, but only after Crook returned with a long beam did Raven calm enough to notice. "What's the-matter, John-nie?"

"I thought you trusted me . . . It doesn't matter, Joe."

"Ahhhh. Ahh-ah-ah." Raven lowered his head. "It was the badness, John-nie. The badness." He picked fuel from his fire. "You-must talk to-the old man. Wake him and tell him Crook is-watching below."

"Well?" Leggatt whispered by the window. "I can goad the frog into laying a real hot one and we could sail out of here in a balloon. If we had a balloon."

"With the dry rot here, his fire is already under the boards."

"So?" Leggatt lit a cigarette. "We dangle over this moat of slivered wine jugs while our Neanderthal friend castrates us with a broken beam end?"

"In half an hour the moon will drop behind that ridge—building. It will be dark enough their own fire will blind them. We'll push the bridging over and cross without a knot."

"John-nie?"

"We've a lot to talk about, Joe. But I'll be down soon."

"Has he signed-yet?"

"That's what we're talking." Leggatt stared into the moon. "You go first, while I keep them busy. Otherwise, we'll drop them your check and chance that."

"Never." DeFord looked below where Crook leaned into the night.

"Cats, Joe!" The beam swung deftly as a broom. "Cats!"

DeFord withdrew behind the protecting sill. Would Johnie betray me? he thought. Not out of knowing. There is little room for it in all that nonsense and extravagance. Tanner swayed into the alley as if on a string, his handsome face sagging heavily as he made water and staggered away. "Damn fool," DeFord said. "Damn fool Tanner."

"So the counselor didn't have a jug under his mattress, after all."

"Damn fool."

"Is it so enormous to want to be—exceptional?"

Raven stirred. "Crook? Light an-other by the window so you-can see better."

"He could have started again."

Smoke thickened the shadows as Raven sang:

"Runs—he runs
old men they run
chase him down
he runs, he-runs"

"Suppose he had a dream? And it was smashed for him?"

"Please, Joe—the floor's getting awfully hot over here, Joe."

"There is more than one way to bridle a horse."

"And, no doubt, to break one. But for practical purposes the horse is extinct. Still, I admire your brush morality. Does it work? Again, for all purposes, experts have taken from Tanner his franchise to your brush morality. Tanner can only read of it in papers. If he wanted to be hero his chance was five years ago, when Raven first put the squeeze on him."

"I can't believe that."

"Then you are a very stupid old man." Leggatt snubbed his cigarette. "I'll tell you what I learned of chance . . . across the world on the Changjin . . . I had kept alive by not relinquishing a dream—no doubt a very young man's dream. A scrap of silk, a souvenir of what I submit is the human condition. And, jurors, peers, judges, I submit this yet . . . My dream was of a young girl. She was a number of things which hardly matter now. And she would vary from day to day. Then the CCP came into it, and that day I shot a little Chinese soldier running at me with a pitchfork. 'Keep moving,' the CO shouted. I stopped. It was a girl. A beautiful thing—about seventeen—new uniform, size too large, tennis shoes, white socks. A volunteer, she'd come a thousand miles from some village somewhere to defend her Asia with a pitchfork. 'Keep moving, Lieutenant!' Sure . . . Her face drained, then her pupils glazed, their points of life withdrew from the cold. Extinguished." A match scratched in Leggatt's hand, burned a smoky hole in the shadows where he absently relit his cigarette. "My captain was running at me—mortars probing from every fucking where—on a rise off a hundred yards, a soldier sat on a little Mongol pony. I remember the sun catching the bugle slung at his neck. He looked once while I stood over the girl. Then he charged. It was fantastic. That little horse bounding like a deer, and the CO scrabbling for his pistol. 'Nail him, Johnie! Nail his ass!' The horse stumbled but bounced up, took a shell hole, and then the dirt shrugged like a tossed blanket, and there was nothing. Direct hit. One of his own, I imagine."

"Can-you see better, Crook? Is-the fire helping?"

"No. Light's bad. I'll get them, Joe."

"Put more wood-on."

"Don't, Joe. Someone will see. Please, Joe, it's awfully hot, Joe."

"Have-a drink, Al-fred. Then shut-up."

DeFord's boots gritted the rubble. "Why are you telling me this?"

"What you said about Tanner. You have lived too long without remembering. You have forgotten that to last, one must sustain oneself with a promise, even if it is a very young man's promise. And from then on, you risk losing the promise. And consequently, everything."

"Listen—" DeFord could not say he wanted Leggatt . . . wanted to touch Leggatt's arm. But he could not bear to have Leggatt hear him fumble in the darkness. After a while he said, "You would have all the fathers go to war and the sons stay home." The darkness deepened between them. "Why must you defend yourself? Who judges you?"

"No one. Which is why I judge myself."

"The girl would have killed you."

"Perhaps she was as innocent as my dream of her."

"She would have killed you."

"I did not kill her bugler, did I?"

DeFord did not answer, and Leggatt went on. "And because I did not, they sent me back, slipped me a medal and flew me quickly home. But they couldn't disengage me from the clerical tape before I crawled the walls—but that's something else. You are not stupid. I shouldn't have said that."

DeFord was thinking: If I measure my strength by the change I have been able to understand, then I have no strength. And if I measure my happiness by the love Johnie has for me—I am empty. Still, I feel neither weak nor empty. Perhaps the measure is how long you can hold on. "No, you did not kill her bugler," he whispered.

"Need light, Joe. Can't see the cats no more."

"Build-it up, Crook."

"I'd best put the bridging across. The moon's down." Leggatt grunted, went to the stairwell and talked with Raven while DeFord slid their bridging out, feeding it over the sill until it rested on the opposite roof.

"Cats, Joe! Cats!"

"You-lied, John-nie. You lied." Raven threw slatting to the fire, and flame curled at Leggatt.

"I wouldn't do that, Joe. You need a permit in this town. Where's your certificate?"

"Bitches! Bitches! Burn him, Joe!"

"Cer-tif-fa-ket! Cert-tif-fi-agg!" Raven hurled wood to the flames. "We don't need-no stink-king cer-tifi-cate!"

Something crashed into the alley. "Johnie?" DeFord called from the opposite rooftop. "The bridging's down!"

"Well, well." Leggatt warmed his hands over the stairwell. "Without a fire permit it's all very illegal. Yet something's sending up smoke. Joe? Is your ass on fire?"

"You-feel alive now, John-nie. A-live?"

"Hurry, Johnie," DeFord called. But Leggatt waited until Crook was forced into the hall, where Proudhomme crouched whimpering. Only Raven moved among the flames, as if charmed. Then Leggatt forced the window wide, climbed the sill, and as DeFord's heart beat in his throat, leaped.

They watched the room fill with flame, and Deford's heart calmed. "With my big shoulders and your big bottom, we'll just fit that roof door, won't we, Johnie?"

"You might have saved my belt."

"I figured a man like you could talk his trousers tight out of sheer admiration." They descended the tenement slowly, Leggatt pounding every door and screaming "fire" in a dozen accents. Well surrounded by tenement people, they passed onto the street. But the trick was unnecessary. As the first of the fire engines maneuvered into position, Raven was absorbed by sound and glitter, his face happy and innocent as a child's.

IX

Now DeFord remembered the staring men in the jungle camp west of a small Wyoming border town when he and the peddler—what was his name? Red Jacks maybe. Yes. He and Jacks stepped off the trestle, slid through the scrub sage, and walked the gulch out a mile to the river. They had not exchanged more than a sentence or two since Denver, they were so tired watching for railroad bulls. Red Jacks said it was getting impossible for a man to make his way. At the jungle camp Jacks whispered, "Tight face, kid. Something's up." A dozen men watched from the shade: like any bunch of hobos DeFord had seen from Michigan to Colorado. But these were not boiling clothes, there no stew fired, no one was passing last week's paper. Jack took vegetables, potatoes, and a can of bully from his pack. A coffee can lay on the wet fire-bed, its bottom shot out, its grounds not yet dry in the ashes. "When'd they come through?"

"About an hour go." A bo in denims boiled white and jungle-sewn on the knees strolled from the shade. "Two bulls, a stoolie, and a deputy scissorbull. Shot up everything cooking and said to rod it by dark. Some fucker slipped into town last night—and robbed a store. Or maybe it was two fuckers." Another bo flanked him, so DeFord stood by Jacks. Nobody said anything for a while, Jacks looking from man to man as they moved from their stump ends to stand by White Denims.

"So you figure if you catch the hijack you'll throw him to the home guard?"

"Fuck the home guard. But this was good diggings—it's twenty miles to the next. They want every man out." White Denims pointed to Jack's blanket roll. "Bindle stiffs too."

"Well, there's still time for a throw together. Where's your chronicker?"

"By the river. He heard them coming—slipped a pot into the brush. Washing off the mulligan now."

"I'll throw my chuck to it. You frisk my bindle while I'm gone if you want."

"We may do that, bo," said White Denims.

Where a spring cut a clay basin and fed a sheet of sweet water into the river, an old man squatted, washing ashes from pieces of stew. He swore steadily but heard them come up behind. "Pitch a hand to this."

They rinsed bits of carrot and turnip. "What you fellers going to do? Wait them out?"

The old man sat on a rock, bony forearms limp on his knees, hands shaking. "I'm no proper stiff," he insisted. "That's what turns my hair. But I can't work no more worth a tin nickel."

"They shoot up your whole works?"

"Just about. I'm not going to be no damn buzzard, though. They left me one pot, and I'll get hold another rig and work a camp somewheres else. What gets to me is I built that damn border town twenty years ago." He wedged his hands between his knees. "The railroad laid iron right up to her; then me and a whole pack of gandys and rust eaters cashed in and built the town. Put her up in six-half weeks. I worked my way. I wasn't no proper stiff."

"You'll be getting by again soon."

"Goddamn town clowns. Damn right I'll be getting by." He watched his hands and did not meet their eyes. "Worked wheat June to November, Texas to Canada," he said to his hands. "Cut ice in winter. Learning to shear sheep down in Arizona—getting pretty fair at it. They shear twicet a year in that country—then some labor shark jawed me to cashing in for the Coast shrimp boats." He lifted his hands from between his thighs. "Goddamn you!" he swore at them. But they still shook.

Jacks and DeFord stood. "We got it thrown together. Where you want the fire?"

"I'll make it. In this dig, it's my job."

White Denims had not looked through the blanket roll, and Jacks was disappointed. "Kind of wished they had, kid. Might clear the air." In the shade the hobos ate slowly, watching, staring, as if something had yet to be righted, as if whatever nomadic mechanisms directing them had failed and they could only wait impotent, womanless, nothing in their packs, nowhere to go. DeFord tried to understand but could not. He was going West to build houses, to send for the girl in Craig. He had promised himself never again to be without money; he would find a place where men were not thrown into scaler ponds or shot down on their own fences. California, Oregon, Washington. It was big country yet.

"Anybody been through New Orleans lately?" Jacks called.

"Yeah. On the bum there. Real tight. Where you been?"

"Through Chicago from New York. They're beefing in Chicago, but things don't look good."

The old man gathered his broken pots. "No matter where you're going, you'd best stay away."

The bos loafed, talking as the food relaxed them. They spoke of the Main Stem in Chicago, of Bughouse Square, of Mother Greenstein's, getting by in winter, days working the iron, mucking trenches, ginking a day here a day there; of jockers and punks, stew bums, buzzards, gay cats, hay bags, gandy stiffs, yard dicks. But always of getting by. As evening came, White Denims set up watches. No one said what he would do if the deputies came. DeFord guessed they did not know themselves. They voted not to lay a fire, and with the darkness each man withdrew to himself. Jacks whispered an escape plan as DeFord stretched under a tree. "I'm sick, kid," Jacks said carefully. "You'll have to get me on my feet if they come." DeFord watched his head slip down on his pack, his body flatten as the earth received it. Hours later he knew the deputies were not coming, but as he lay back exhausted, he knew the men with White Denims were fully awake, staring into the shadows at nothing. In the branches above him, the stars passed like pebbles through handfuls of broken fingers.

He found Jacks at the spring just after daybreak. There was yet crispness in the false shadows, but the air promised heat and the birds already sounded lazy and fat. Jacks was shaving without soap, rinsing the whisker slick into the runover and deliberately kneading his face ahead of the blade. His breathing had a little moan in it. "Know something, kid? Nowadays people die of heart attack, miner's lung, cancer, all sorts. But in the old days a man had a better break—it was either the pains or the fevers —none of this other trash." As he lifted his throat to the razor his eyes winced, then smiled. "Things are not like they were in the old days—and never were. Don't you forget that." While DeFord used the razor, Jacks took seeds from a cloth bag and planted them carefully in a loamy patch above the spring. "Grapes," he answered when DeFord pointed. "Wild grapes."

At camp they boiled coffee and reheated a portion of mulligan. Only the chronicker was awake. "I figured it," the old man said. "Last night I figured it perfect. Going to town and get me another chronicker setup. Going to go right this morning. Maybe I'll recognize someone—maybe someone will remember me. Twenty years isn't that long. It'll work perfect. You think it'll work?"

"It might at that." Jacks trimmed his pack, and the three of them walked the gully back, scrabbling up the trestle. There was no heat in the bed, but to the east the tracks narrowed white under the lifting sun.

"Where you boys headed?" The old man seemed to have lost his directions.

"West Coast." Jacks pointed where the tracks plunged.

"I'm going into town and get me another setup." The old man did not move.

"You'll be getting by again soon," Jacks said carefully. "Thanks for the use of your camp. It was real nice."

"Your chuck beef was good . . . Say, think I should go back and wake the boys before I head to town?"

"They'll be up when they've got something to get up for."

"Guess."

They left him standing there and walked a mile of ties to the watering tank; four days later they were outside Seattle, resting by a fence. "So you're heading down to California?" Jacks selected a sunny place just outside the plowing line, cast a few grape seeds and covered them with a trickle of earth. "Rain any day now. These might just take hold."

"Why do you carry those seeds?"

"To see where I've been, ever I care to come back again . . . Luck to you, kid. You might think about getting a bit of a stake before you go south. Enough to coach it. Making the rods is getting tight . . . See that farm over there? That's where I'll start. Sharpening scissors, mending pots, fixing sewing machines—peddling a thing or two."

"Have you been at it long?"

"Four years in the federal prison outside of Jersey City. This will be my first venture into the business world." Inexplicably he turned away and swore hard and long, then just as suddenly turned back, grinning. "Say, I got something for you, kid." He reached for his pack, and DeFord opened his hand, but Jacks only swung the pack to his shoulders. "Something I learned in Jersey City. Take one day at a time, kid. Got that?"

DeFord nodded. "Why were you—"

"I didn't want to go to war, that's why. And besides, they got the finest sewing-machine-repair course on God's green earth."

◇ ◇ ◇

Leggatt and DeFord entered the Village on Washington Place. "That piece of action couldn't have set me better for looking up Frank. Lately I find it necessary to precede a responsibility with a victory. You seem tired. Let's sit a minute."

DeFord allowed himself to be maneuvered to a bench facing the eastern Bowery approaches. Under the city's bluish neon caul, they could not distinguish the Mulberry fire, but one siren wail reached them through the separating canyons as Leggatt spread himself and gazed into the trees. "Not everyone could have come whole from that spot, so now's my strongest time to look up my brother and con my winter's stake."

"Must you take it?"

"I've left six jobs since the war. Each time the boss, manager—whatever—offered a promotion. Finally a letter of recommendation. I never particularly wanted to get out. I had to." Leggatt stared at Bowery. "There is always a time when work seems to interfere with learning, pleasure, life. It appears most people find relatively successful solutions. Evidently work takes an especially nasty attitude toward me. Just when I believe I'm lost to the crowd, work hauls me out and bashes my sanity on the nearest curb. Quite howling mad, I stumble into my job and have to quit before I do something irreparable. So I have to have my brother's money. The perils of Mulberry and you make it easier."

DeFord planned to explain the spike, for he thought Leggatt would be pleased to know he could have escaped alone. Now wasn't Leggatt saying he needed to be depended upon, needed him, DeFord?

"What are you smiling about?"

"Beginning to be rested."

Whistling through his teeth, Leggatt led them across the square to a small restaurant, whose headwaiter immediately blocked their way. "Service entrance."

"Kitchen," Leggatt sallied, side-stepping while the waiter futilely waved his velvet menu at the bar boy. Leggatt came to bay in a pantry corner and helped himself to a breadstick. "Is Frank Leggatt around?" With a crackle of linen and silk, the headwaiter sank back, received in his world of leather, candlelight and Muzak by a brittle arpeggio of laughter. Almost instantly a round man appeared, as if flung, fully cologned, from the polished woodwork. Leggatt chose his second breadstick and smiled. "A bit stale."

"They're yesterday's. For the help."

"Of course. Has Frank been in yet?"

"Anything I can do? Sandwich, drink?"

"I'm John, Frank's brother."

"So!" A hand bound in silk and weighted by a gold walnut link swung up to be shaken. "Why on earth didn't you say?" The headwaiter burst in with a policeman, but the gold walnut paddled the air. "Misunderstanding, Officer. Nice of you to drop by; I happen to have an extra sirloin. See the salad man." The policeman twirled his night stick, established his authority and withdrew with the sirloin.

"You do resemble Frank."

"I haven't seen my brother in months. How is he?"

The owner grasped his gold walnuts and rocked on his heels. "Touch of Midas, Mr. Leggatt. A genius, your brother."

Leggatt pinched breadsticks before selecting. "Expect him soon?"

"He's just left—incredible fellow. You know how long he took to inventory tonight? Fifteen minutes. And his bar tally . . ." He sucked his stomach, lifting imaginary coffee to his lips while measuring a row of pots. "One long look at the bottles—he estimated eight hundred and forty-six dollars. We made count—eight hundred and forty-three! And those pickled beans. Who'd have known they'd be the talk. The talk of the City?"

"Frank."

"But let me show you something." He drew them to the observation port. "See that fellow there? Gene Shelton. And there—at the canapés—Maurice Ewalk."

"I'm damned."

"The very one. And with him, Kreplun, the painter. He and your brother dined together."

Leggatt squinted. "Kreplun?"

"Which reminds me." The owner signaled his bar boy to refill their glasses. "Your brother's plan. Men like Shelton, Ewalk, Kreplun—make them feel at home."

Leggatt searched velveteen surfaces. "Damned. Plastic tie—portable circus and all. Must still be hustling for Frank."

"They have business together. Later. It is said some talents run in families. You wouldn't happen—"

"No, I lack all of Frank's creativity. Sometimes these things are distributed quite unevenly."

"Yes. I suppose these are compensations. We can't all—"

"After they made Frank they lost the mold."

The owner nodded, studied Leggatt as if to assess his weight in breadsticks, and sighed. "Frank's brother. I never would . . . I'll tell him you dropped by."

Leggatt chose a last stick before moving toward the alley. "Do that." He walked with hands hidden in his rear pockets. "Kreplun. This late in the day. Still in drag. Business with Frank. Needs him, portable camp and all. Now why—?"

"Is your brother an accountant?"

"What? No. No . . . I sense things, DeFord. Kreplun tonight. My brother dangling his two hundred and fifty dollars. One look and I know. I smell my brother trying to use me." He brightened.

"I figured it would be something about holding a job."

"Impossible."

◇ ◇ ◇

"Hey, Johnboy." The longest car DeFord had ever seen pulled up next to them. As its rear window slipped noiselessly down, a soft light was mirrored on a surface of mahogany, and a gray-haired man leaned forward from dark leather cushions, his tapered gloves limp in his square hand. "Long time, Johnboy. How have you been?"

Leggatt leaned on the window frame. "Fine, Mr. Nicholas. You don't look too well. Been sick?"

Mr. Nicholas' trimmed pepper-and-salt brows spread over his eyes. "Ah, Johnboy. Everyone's been telling me I look fine. When I saw you, I knew I'd get the truth. Like a mirror. A mirror." He eased to the window, smiling warmly at DeFord. Then he reached back; a young man raised himself from a corner and produced a roll of Tums. Still appraising DeFord, Mr. Nicholas slipped a Tums between his even white teeth, smiled and cracked it to slivers. "Forty years of her home-baked sandwiches, I told my dentist. Good hard-crusted old-country lunches. My teeth are the best he's seen. It's all in the gums." The short neck turned in its silk collar. "But the rest, Johnboy. Too much work, too much worry. Had a hatful of intestine taken out at St. Vincent's last month. 'Noodles,' she calls it. 'My boy had his noodles trimmed.' "

"How is Mrs. Nicholas?"

"Lovelier than ever. Hey? What you think of my office? Her idea. Keep me off my feet for a while . . . By the way"—he returned the Tums to his young man—"my nephew Victor."

"Evening." Victor showed his perfect teeth.

Mr. Nicholas' handsome eyebrows shrugged. "Excuse. Victor has an examination tomorrow. Don't worry so, Victor. *Quando il lavoro é poco, Vittorio, la vita é lunga* . . . Now go across to Mrs. Makum's and ask after her. Three flights up. Second apartment."

Victor climbed out, smoothing his dark cashmere. "What should I say?"

"Just pass some time—pass some time. And buy another

of those stomach things . . . Ah, Johnboy. Too much work. You know Mrs. Makum? A fine woman. Trouble with her pension. But it's all been settled. Where you living now?"

"Under the Williamsburg Bridge."

"Eh? What ward you vote?"

"I don't vote."

Mr. Nicholas shook his head. "Everyone should vote. It's a duty . . . Hey, what you think of my nephew? Quiet tonight, but he's a good boy. Got himself a new convertible, nice apartment uptown, little cottage upstate—"

"What's he do?"

"Do? He's a senior at Fordham." Nicholas showed his teeth. "But what should I care? Last term he would have made Dean's List—except for his language course . . . Under a bridge, eh? You looking for a job?"

"Just showing my friend the town. He's from Oregon."

"Oregon?" He studied DeFord. "Teamster? What local?"

"Carpenter. I'm not a union man."

Nicholas clicked his teeth. "Everybody should join a union. It's a duty." He smiled. "Well, it takes all kinds. You change your mind before you go back, look me up."

Leggatt rubbed his nose. "*Zio* Nick, you old bastard, who do you know in Oregon?"

Nicholas laughed. "Even in Oregon, Johnboy. I know people even in Oregon."

The smiling Victor returned and offered a cup of ice cream. "She says everything's fine. She says you're a saint, and God bless you. She sent this."

"Ah. Spumoni. But I'll just take a Tums. Ask Louis if he wants some spumoni."

The boy lifted the chauffeur's intercom. "Louis? You want—"

"Use the language, Vittorio! *Parla in italiano!*"

Victor shrugged. *"Luigi?"* He struggled. *"Vorresti . . . qualche gelato?"*

"Non 'qualche' . . . 'un' gelato," Mr. Nicholas corrected.

"Va bene, vorresti un gelato."

"Jesus Mary," Nicholas said to Leggatt. "He's got the accent of a Sicilian garlic farmer. How the hell those professors expect him to learn if they don't make him practice?" One instant his teeth were smiling, the next his face went hard as marble. He leaned forward. "I've always liked you, Johnboy. You need a few bucks?"

"Thanks, Nick. Thanks, but no."

The suede gloves described a languorous arc. *"Dunque, non tutte le strade portano à Roma."* He turned; his stubby hand grabbed his nephew's neck and shook it caressingly. "Now tell Louis to take us down Carmine Street, careful of the stop signs. And if you don't get it right, I just may take away the convertible . . . See you, Johnboy. My regards to your brother."

◇ ◇ ◇

"Anything wrong?" Leggatt reached for DeFord and guided him along the sidewalk. "Were you thinking about Uncle Nick?"

"No. Is your brother some sort of accountant?"

"You've already asked. So you were thinking of Nicholas. You shouldn't. It's his charm that's most disturbing. Gets you wondering all sorts of things. Which is why I never touch his money."

"Your brother doesn't work with him, then?"

"No. Yes. Frank is neither for nor against Mr. Nicholas. And so he works with him. For Nicholas, you may or may not work with him, as you choose. Against, of course, you do not. But in between you are working with him."

"You are against."

"Not at all. I'm for Mr. Nicholas. But I won't work with him. I'm for bank robbers, draft dodgers, moonshiners, smugglers, using the mails for any material: seditious, treasonous or obscene; most grand larceny—but especially bank robbers."

"But you don't do any of those things."

"I can't take the responsibility."

For a full minute DeFord tried sincerely to remember when living had seemed so easily judged. He could not. "How many places does your brother work?" he asked as Leggatt led him back to Washington Square.

"As many as he can. Frank takes close to one hundred thousand a year out of this city."

One hundred thousand, DeFord thought. Dollars. Dollars? Yes, but whenever he heard that much money, it came slow to think it was the same money he made. As if the man who made that much did not actually draw it in dollars, but in something called dollars. He knew exactly what he could get with a dollar, remembered working all day to make just one—big things then, half the size of a shake shingle. But they printed them smaller after a while, and he was paid five or six a day, then gradually to twenty or twenty-five. But a hundred thousand runs almost four hundred each working day. He pursed his lips. Had he that breed of money he would slip up to Portland, where an outfit made the best working boots in the world. Sixty dollars a pair. A man really needed two pair, since boots last three times as long if you let them rest between shifts. But still, that was only one hundred twenty, and this other was a hundred thousand. It certainly was uphill to think of that as money. "A lot of inch and a half."

"It's all time and a half." Leggatt guided among the Square strollers. "Mile and a half with Frank—sit down, quick! Don't look around—we'll talk here for a while. Keep your face hidden."

DeFord obeyed, his heart beginning to swell under his lungs. "Raven?"

"Proudhomme. But he's dressed like a Fifth Avenue faggot. Now just what the hell is Joe up to?" He lay his face into his hands, pretending exhaustion. "Hasn't seen us yet. But if Perversion's here, can Death be far behind?"

"Can't we turn about and walk out the way we came in?"

"Certainly. First I'd like to see what scene he's making."

"Hear me. What does he want?"

"He wants your pension check."

"Boondoggle!" DeFord felt his anger in a ribbon at the root of his heart, and he wanted to tear it out in long strips, filling himself until he could seek Raven and—"That's not what he wants," he made himself say.

"No. He wants you. And perhaps were we to think long enough or simply be damn plain lucky, we would understand. But I don't think so. Do you . . . ? I guess you don't. So let's talk something else."

"Then tell me about your brother."

"Oh Jesus, that's worse. I suppose I've asked for it." He lighted a cigarette. "Whenever I'm faced with Frank, I never know where to begin. Perhaps it's a biochemical enigma: even given similar environments, the varieties of behavior are infinite. What is same environment . . . ? I'll start again: my brother and I never fought, never disagreed. Yet we have as much in common as a fox and a buffalo. Still, I suppose we have everything in common. The first emissary from another galaxy will no doubt look upon our species as you or I would see a Dutchman's tulip garden. No, not what I want to say . . . Start three: since I can remember, my brother has collected facts. What is your name, where do you live, what do you do, price of this, distance here to there, cost of, weight, number. Let me describe his mind. Its entire surface freckled with facts—billions of cells pickling the markets, trends, weights, distances—fourteen hundred cubic centimeters of whitish pulp eager to absorb and store. For the last ten years Frank has had the same thought at the close of each day: Have I made my four hundred dollars? If not, he gets on his phone, racing the sun, calling cross-country to friends, markets, businesses—until he has traded, bargained, exchanged whatever is to be traded, bargained, exchanged. Only then he takes himself to bed. But that is insufficient . . . Start four: facts, graphs, labels serve Frank as culture, art, morality, philosophy, religion serve most of us." He drew on his cigarette. "But the damn thing is, we're twins. Identical. He's five minutes older than I. Oh yes, he keeps a mustache, about forty pounds more weight, and wears very handsome clothing. The conclusion I inevitably reach is none of this means a watery damn. But yet . . . but yet . . ."

"Why must you measure it?"

"Measure? I can't get past wondering it. But there is a measure." Leggatt laid a dollar bill between them. "For the last year I've been living, after my painting expenses, on twelve of these each week. Laid end to end would be . . ."

"Two yards."

"Two paces. The last time I visited Frank he had an exceptional week: ninety-five hundred twenty-two dollars."

"Fifteen hundred eighty-seven paces."

"Really? From this bench, it's about that distance to Bowery. Less up Fifth to Frank's town house . . . You're very fast with figures."

"Something I have had to use, so I'm handy."

"Tell me, what makes a good carpenter? What is a good carpenter?"

"If you build a roof, for example—you use the best wood available, trim always on the weathered ends, and if she is kiln-dried, you match side grains best possible, to allow for warp. And then there is the studdings—you want your studdings spaced perfect so—"

"But the roofing is covered with tar paper and sheeting. No one will ever see your work. No one will ever know."

"I will."

"That's a measure." Leggatt folded the dollar. "Yes, that is a measure, all right."

X

Sauterne lies heavy in Dee Bee Smith, metal sweet on his tongue and beautifully dull behind his eyes, although a sour blade of it whets the very bottom of his stomach. Nevertheless, headache is gone. Everything, he thinks. All there. Fresh clothing lies folded beside him in the packing case, and the wine warmth has brought all into order. No longer a tangle of responsibility, tomorrow's clothes are simply "Disguise," and the promise to deliver a package for the pear-shaped spy is part of "Plan." Everything is one.

Sauterne works its second phase as the warmness ebbs, recalling hunger. Yet Dee Bee is flooded with generosity as if his every cell knows to the swallow that much more wine remains. "Perhaps it was the shower as well," he says to his bottle, remembering the shower in the Chinaman's store and shaving while the Chinaman washed his clothes. The water made his eyes sting and his bottom itch. But he will be clean tomorrow, when he passes into plan, wearing disguise. "Memo: Each thing belongs to everything." Generosity teases toward confidence, and he thinks: The Respectables will not know. They will be tricked. The weight of his confidence pulls at his stomach, and he winces. Quickly. Bottle.

The basement is dark, soundless, but he knows where each part of disguise lies, and beneath him feels the warmth in the newspaper ticking of his packing crate. A good place. He drifts toward sadness as the blade twists and his eyes begin to water in protest. My last night here. Everything goes. Block has been good to me. More than I deserved. Dee Bee crawls from his paper nest and enters the alley. At the alley mouth he looks from corner to corner of his beloved block. Sauterne is good for headaches but makes you sad. Port for hunger but brings bad dreams. Muscatel for sleep. Sherry dries you out; Chianti makes you sweat. Burgundy for warmth but morning shakes. None alone is perfect. Still, a decision for wine is best. He starts along the sidewalk carefully, wanting to walk block at night one last time. However, when he reaches Elizabeth and Houston he has accepted the sourness and decides rather than walking block he will contemplate block. So he climbs a tenement and finds a corner on the roof where he can study the quiet part, Elizabeth part of the block.

Above hangs the city's neon caul, but Dee Bee has eyes only for his own block's rooftops, rediscovering beloved outlines as chimney pots and television aerials shatter the grayness. A large shadow glides close, and roosting pigeons rustle and coo. "Owl," Dee Bee says, making inventory. He has seen them before: huge tuft-eared things perched by day in shadows, hunting the city by night. Staring where the owl disappeared, Dee Bee sees movement and glitter.

Two blocks west on Mulberry Street a pack of fire engines wail down from the north, while orange, smokeless flames crawl the skyline. Dee Bee sips sauterne and finds himself remembering patches of when he was a whiskey lush. The days and nights of it have been stirred and poured into one memory upon which a few images float. But he remembers the overall feeling whiskey gave. A sort of courage. Recalling such times, not specifically, but with the memory of that sense of courage, Dee Bee shakes his head. He giggles. The whiskey, he realizes, made him walk the city, kept him moving tortuously. You are not that way, bottle. Yes, wine is true, whiskey false. Stupid days, his whiskey days. Their memory recedes, leaving a thin spoor of confusion. He blinks and counts the television aerials on block. More and more blue boxes each year. But it is not surprising. They are coming, isn't it so? Dee Bee sips and leans over the edge of the roof.

Careful! Danger! Below on Elizabeth a long limousine crawls the corner and stops. A young man steps out, smooths his coat and leans toward a rear window. A pair of gloves flickers; the young man nods and walks the sidewalk, glancing into alleys, up stairways. The black car follows, stops when the young man has studied the block; the young man reenters; the limousine returns toward Village.

The men who will deliver the package for the spy, Dee Bee thinks, leaping to the truth of it out of brute cunning alone, for the entire complex of They, spy, package and Respectables is too much horror for him to pick at. Yes. It could only be that. His senses—plunging toward the plexus of possible cause and probable effect, plunging toward the skein of respectability—rebel and jerk to nothing. His hand finds silk, his lips bottle, and for a long time he strokes and sucks.

His body craves wine, yet the part of him that still re-

tains its cunning knows he must first conclude. He has too much to lose: plan, disguise, escape from pursuing Respectables. All rewards will be his. He can afford, therefore, to hold back this once and bear the pain of reasoning it out. The swine. It must be this way: the Respectables have sent their spy, and their spy wants him to accept a package and bring it to him. The Respectables in the great black car could just as easily give this package to their spy outright. The pain of it. Why do they need him? Why must he—?

Heh heh heh heh. The cleverness. The simplicity. They want him to take a job, to take responsibility, to accept delivery of the package, then daily delivery of something, and then all and all that follows. They want him to return to whiskey, to drink whiskey again as They all do. And to feel the false courage They all feel because of their whiskey. Heh heeee hee. He pulls sauterne to him and whispers to it: "Memo: Dee Bee Smith is no such fool."

Dee Bee cradles his wine and stares out over his beloved block. The plan to escape was made in the very nick. Had it not been for the old lumberjack, he never would have gotten the first fiver and never would have been able to purchase disguise, et cetera, et cetera. He allows the sense of fortune to soak into his brain, and there, with a few sips of wine to brace it, he garners the strength to consider even further the plans the Respectables have for him. Oh yes. They want him to start again: responsibility, whiskey, false courage. Well, he will deliver their package in the morning, and then when They think They have him, he'll slip away and escape, disguised as one of Them.

Bottle empty—the swine, he thinks; they upset me so poor bottle would not hold to it—Dee Bee Smith moves once again toward a grogshop. Almost closing time. But I'll make it. The idea of an extra bottle, a treat, makes him very happy. As he shuffles along he dreams of a new block, a new and unknown block where the Respectables will never find him. And he realizes again that without the old lumberjack, none of it would have been possible.

Perhaps I shall deliver the package to the old lumberjack, he thinks. He wants a respectable job. Perhaps he can use their money. It would be nice to do something for him, now wouldn't it?

◇ ◇ ◇

Only when threatened did DeFord feel the insult of losing and remember those DeFords of his *Carpenter's Manual,* Ithaca, Michigan, Craig. Only when tired and alone did he remember the breed poacher and his own terror as he recognized the bleached lattice under the pilot's jacket. During his years of following contract to contract, he had never truly known the usual fears, those sudden winter fears that slip in even where the settled man sits content, drunk by his stove. Mostly DeFord remembered places. Now, sitting on the Village bench, he wondered if such would not someday be the same with Leggatt. Even Leggatt might forget the girl soldier, forget Elizabeth Street, maybe forget his anger and disgust. It would take a long while. As Codgers said, Johnie was always at war. Foreign and domestic. You can not be at war with land, can not be at war with unseen places always ahead whenever you seek change. But Leggatt was home guard, scissorbull. Everyone was home guard now. And now my heart has me wintering this city, I'm home guard as well, he thought. Yet except for Raven, the city had not put his back to a tree as it had with Leggatt. Perhaps once you have to winter the city, you must keep one city-jump ahead of whatever will tree you. What had treed Johnie? Whiskey? No. Something about his painting, something about the man Kreplun, something about his brother. It was odd how whatever possible city-thing might get to a man would, by and by. Raven: the threat of defilement, the horror of dying without—dignity. And such had come within a city-month. It was all loose-mouthed to believe Raven had sought him out, yet he could not help it. Sometimes he suspected city-things did seek a man out. No matter, he thought. I have my place and have had many places—not wars, domestic or foreign, but places I can remember.

Next to him Leggatt lit a cigarette, and across the square an old pacifist's banner caught a breeze, while a crowd watched its master perform. Cats, Joe. Cats! DeFord remembered, his mind slipping free to places, high-country places.

◇ ◇ ◇

The rainbow trout is a true salmon. Maybe that is why you can fish it anywhere. He had caught rainbows in Colorado up mountain from Red Feather, where beaver wove mud and logs to hold the snow water. Once he caught over sixty in under an hour, by tying a black gnat to a number-fourteen barbless hook. He liked barbless fishing, especially in high water overstocked with the silver, red-streaked true salmon. In open water—millponds outside Portland and Seattle—dry flies were the sport. Once he landed a rainbow over twenty-five inches—twelve pounds it weighed—and because he left his net on the bank, he gaffed it through mouth and gills. By the time he walked the logs to shore the rainbow had flayed against his leg so, it was the summer's end before his thumb healed. Yes, he caught rainbow many places. And Eastern brook in the high lakes—fine pretty things, good fighters; but he tired of the way they kept to bottom and tended to school up. And German brown were a lot of trout. Great underslung jaw and often real mean. It was a good thing to play in something both beautiful and ugly. But in Western water the brown favored big lakes, while DeFord chose the high streams, where things were always changing and you never knew what you might find at the next riffle. He fished the Kokanee too. It was good trout, but not like the cutthroat. And grayling, Dolly Varden, jack salmon, steelhead, the whole creel. But none were like the cutthroat. Cutthroat were native. You could say most salmon were native—certainly the rainbow—but when you said native trout, you meant cutthroat; you meant the small unbelievably beautiful fish that fought up the mountain riffles each spring, where they near starved in the high icy pools. The only trout they might abide was the rainbow, but even then it was rare you found them sharing a hole of milky snow water.

DeFord smiled. Yes, cutthroat would whittle himself to nothing but fight and hunger, swimming to the very source of mountain water, once he figured a pool was too small to be shared. No hard feelings. DeFord imagined the cutthroat respected the rainbow—since rainbow were kin to the big chinook salmon—and the chinook was too much fish even for cutthroat to snub. But cutthroat felt there was room enough for everyone, and would just as leave go it alone, though in the high famished places he seldom grew ten inches before marten or bear or ice got him. The only stretch DeFord had caught many cutthroat in with rainbow was the Seven Mile Hole of the Yellowstone. And they were big too. Heavy as hatchery brook. But the Yellowstone was a queer place—everything overfed, with the wildness tamed out and the bear as fat as house dogs.

The largest cutthroat he caught was at Glass Creek the summer he built a way camp for a timber survey crew. That was Diamond Peak country, he remembered. In August, Glass Creek was so clear it could not be fished except for very small poaching trout—best eating, anyway. One evening he went with the crew to see the big one everybody had tried. Salmon eggs, flies, nymphs, bait —one timber beast even attempted that trick of floating a mouse on a shake, then jerking the mouse off. DeFord peered over boulders into a blue crystal of water so clear he saw the caddis nymphs moving on its bottom. Under the lens of water in the lower quadrant, the big trout looked the length of his arm.

"Might as well be painted on the bottom, for all the raises I've got of him," one of the crew said.

"It's getting your gear to float right," said the youngest. "Water's so glassy you let your line drag a hair and you spook him. If you could slip close enough to keep your tip high and then float a hare's-ear—"

"You might get a raise with a blue dunn," the first said. "But no hare's-ear this high."

"Who brought a rod?" asked DeFord.

The Swede trail man laughed. "I packed one. It's getting pretty sorry when these sports tramp three miles just to look at a fish."

"May I use it?"

"It's not mine. My sporting's in the fall." He propped his elbows over his knees. "Never wanted to work twenty years trying to be half as smart as a fish."

"It's my pole. I guess I forget it in camp." The youngest rolled a cigarette. "You know, I'd give you that pole just to see you raise him."

"Not in his pool. He knows every turn of water. Even were you to manage proper drift, he would not take it." DeFord snuck to the pool above, caught two small cutthroat on salmon eggs, and used the largest hook the crew could find in their pockets to mount a thumb-size piece of trout meat. Then with the rod strapped to a log, its line cinched with a yard of slack, he went to the second pool above the big fish, chopped the remaining cutthroat, and tied its meat into his handkerchief. The crew watched from the rocks as he dipped and kneaded the handkerchief. He could not see the water below, but he had only to lift his head to see the rod tip.

"He's lifting," the Swede said.

"Whoo—whee, he's a coming!"

Yes, DeFord thought. Cannibal. And now he can't bear the notion of another cannibal just one pool atop of him tearing up a young one, so he will bust out—

"Damn but that fish looks mean."

Yes. If you can't get them hungry, get them mad. With a flinch of pleasure he saw the rod tip bend, tighten, and dance, so he scrambled to unlash it and play his fish. When the crew reached him, the young one blew through his teeth. "I sure favored that pole. But your trick was worth it."

DeFord said nothing until it was apparent the big one was not going to strip line thirty yards downstream over snags, but bulldog right where he was. Then he turned to the boy. "I don't want your gear. Just bank that fish. He'll eat a hundred times his weight in fry before something gets to him." The boy knew his rod well: he let the fish fight the taper of bamboo until he rolled on his side, and the Swede waded the snow water to hand-gaff him.

The cannibal went twenty-five inches. Probably a record for nonsea-run cutthroat, they figured. Then they all got excited and hungry, caught a dozen poachers and broiled them on green switches. DeFord and the boy ate the big one.

"I hunt the quail." The Swede sat Indian fashion and studied DeFord. "If you're in this country September, you look me up. I've got something you'll like."

The something was a Parker .20-gauge double, so light and balanced DeFord learned to simply look where he wanted to shoot, throw the Parker up, and squeeze. He got very fast on quail, but never as good as the Swede, whose Browning automatic would have three birds dead in the air two or three times a season.

DeFord stretched on the Village bench and stared toward Bowery, seeing nothing. Yes, that was a fine piece, that Parker.

"If a tree don't fall on me
I'll live till I die—"

the Swede sang one evening after making a double on blue grouse. DeFord remembered the hillside, each shadow and rock, the Swede dancing down a slide, caulks cracking sparks in the dusk.

"She said, 'I can see you are a logger
by the way you stir your coffee
with your thumb.' "

Yes, that had been good country where the Swede taught him bird hunting. But then Pope and Talbot and Weyerhauser went in and started patch-cutting until the mountains seemed moth-eaten. Splotchy. Well, you had to side houses with something. But still. Even if the clear cuts were good for mountain quail, DeFord had an offer to build some summerhouses, and wanting again to put his hands to skilled finishing, he went north into Mount Hood country.

⬦ ⬦ ⬦

"It's a measure," Leggatt repeated. "That's a measure, all right." His eyes ranged as if seeking a switch to snap the square into darkness. "I've lost Proudhomme. Which may mean he has found us. No matter." DeFord relinquished the high country to walk with Leggatt among cliques of beards and knots of perfumed boys. "What are you grinning about?"

"That fellow looks ready to pitch a bomb."

"He should be so lucky. That's what I like about robbing a bank. Real robbers, real police, real bullets."

"Real money."

"I'll settle for the two hundred and fifty. It will do for a wheat-germ winter. With Sunday dinners at Ma Codgers', Did you ever live on nothing but nuts and berries? Great for the Blake in you. Eventually you loose your appetite, your stomach shrivels, and you have visions."

"I once made a bad year on molasses and cracked barley." He could remember the place, nothing more, not even the taste of the stuff. And he had thought he would never forget. Well, places were best. "But that was in the thirties, and I was in my thirties too. So it was not much of a chore."

"And you had a lot of company."

"Yes, I had a lot of company."

XI

They crossed Waverly Place and mounted the steps of a large brownstone. "Can we go in here dressed this way?"

"Especially this way. It will probably be the same party I staggered out of three years ago." Leggatt led DeFord into a wide hall that separated four high-ceilinged rooms, all with sliding doors. Each was filled with art and artifacts, and contained its own small bar past which people wandered north, west, south, east, squaring the circle with a drink in their hands. Halfway along the tunnel of hallway, the ceiling lifted to the roof, over which a glass dome arched, suggesting a great smashed crystal held by the bind of piece upon broken piece. A circular stairway clung at the edge of this pit, insinuating itself to the second floor, where it wrapped once about the core of the house and came to rest.

A man guarded these stairs, brows contracting to a ledge

of welted tissue over one brown eye and another the color of shale slate.

"Hello, Les. I'm John Leggatt, remember?"

"Sorry, Johnie. I must have been . . ." He offered his hand. "You look in damn good shape." He reached, squeezed DeFord's shoulder and pointed up the stairway. "Last time I saw Johnie he was coming down there, shouting the top of his voice. A hundred people in this hall all shock still, and not one could look at another. He sure turned everybody off."

"Just a moment ago I thought you were ready to lay me out for it."

"Hell no. I didn't understand a word you said . . . No. I suppose I was hoping for a little action. Your friend here's got a good pair shoulders. Hell. Even when something starts, it never starts. It's . . . you know. How you figure who to rush when they're throwing punches over a piece a canvas or some gimcrack?"

"Sounds like the same party."

"Yeah. But the kids are three years older. Say, they missed you, Johnie. Why don't you go up top?"

"Would you see if you can find my brother, Les?"

"I'll tell him you're in the nursery."

Upstairs, a dozen children had collected in a large room overlooking the square. The older ones had glasses of punch; the smaller children sat with poster paints and decorated sheets of paper. "It's amusing," DeFord's self-appointed hostess of seven years explained, "but not necessarily productive." She escorted DeFord to a sideboard and offered tomato juice. "Do you sculpt? I mean, you appear as if you might. They do heavy work, you know."

"I build houses in Oregon."

"You're the first builder of houses of Oregon I've met." She studied the contents of her glass. "Is it rewarding work? Do important people live in Oregon houses, or the masses?"

"Mostly lumber people. Choker setters, whistle punks, timber beasts. Sometimes I build for the mill officers. But I have not met many masses lately."

"The phrase is rather archaic, isn't it? What's a whistle punk?"

"The man who works the whistle on the winch that pulls the logs to the trucks. His whistle signals the choker-setter. Before gas machinery, mules dragged the logs on sleds. So the winch is called a donkey."

"That's very clever. The names, I mean. An overrating of the visual . . . Do you believe a person has to devote himself to something? My father recently gave up a very lucrative business to devote himself to encouraging unrecognized talent. But I have not yet chosen what I shall commit my energies to." She looked steadily into DeFord's eyes. "They tell me I have a great deal of time left to discover myself. In the tests last week at school they said I was an exceptional child."

"You're the first exceptional child I've met."

She gestured, seemed unsatisfied and repeated the movement until it suited her. "Oh, actually we're all of us exceptional children. We have to be. I mean we study for the tests and all. That's why we go to our special school. To be exceptional children. What does an Oregon house look like—is it like brick, or fiberglass?"

"Oregon is a place, not a material."

Her mouth pulled down, but her eyes tilted upwards. "Oh. I'm not being very exceptional this evening, am I?"

"It's uphill work."

"Thank you. That's nice of you to say. And clever too."

The smaller children had gathered about a playhouse where Leggatt hid. As they took turns pulling open the door, he leaped at them. "Ahh sooo. Am Faceless Grabatchu, the Yokohama Strangler!" He reached at a small child. "You will kindly extend your neck, please?"

"That's John, isn't it? Last time he was here we played that game. But I was four then."

Leggatt's face appeared at the playhouse window, his eyes wild. "Gut away fro'm the co'ttage door. C. Weed MacSlime will ta'ke you back to Loch Ness with hum. Ut's cold where he lives—and the wa'ters threy hundrud feet deep!" He hid again from screams and giggles.

"I remember him being more amusing. Perhaps it's only as I no longer like to be frightened. I think a lot about fear, you know."

DeFord sipped tomato juice as Leggatt crept out again. "Vot's dis, my boy needs to eating more green vegetables? You don't come to the right house, maybe? My name Mortify Freesemup, butcher of Tel Aviv—my son need green vegetables, ech? So pickles ain't green?"

"Yes," DeFord said. "They like to be frightened."

"Because they know it's not real." The girl reached to him. "Can you guess what I'm honestly afraid of?"

But were it to become real, he thought. What happens when—?

"Go ahead," the small face below demanded. "Guess."

"That . . . that you might . . . not grow up fast enough?"

"Oh no. I'd like that. What I'm afraid of"—she pulled his sleeve to her—"I won't be exceptional."

"Nothing's easy. You must be angry. You must stay angry."

Her hand tightened on his sleeve. "Are you someone's grandfather? Could you have been someone's grandfather?"

"Ahh. Yes, I suppose I could have been someone's grandfather."

Leggatt came at them, dragging one leg, which had a

small boy wrapped around it. "May we join you? Hello, Rhondi."

The girl's eyes tilted, her voice dropped. "Hello, John."

"A muse! Ah, Rhondi, you've broken my heart. I thought muses uncurled full grown from an egg at seventeen and stayed seventeen until they were forty-three, when they faded into an October sunset."

Rhondi said nothing.

"How wise. But give me none of your silent poisons to drink." Leggatt flourished his leg where the child clung. "Allow me to introduce a fast friend."

"That's Norman. He's a genius."

"So that's why he clings so. Or is it opposites which attract? Listen, Norman, who said you were a genius? You don't have to take that kind of thing from anyone, see?"

"John, you haven't changed at all."

"I certainly have, Rhondi. But it's all too subtle for the uninitiated. Be satisfied I have returned with genius clinging to me like a barnacle. Rather mute, isn't he?"

"Norman doesn't talk. But he reads and writes and sketches beautifully. And his scores on the tests run off the graphs."

Leggatt stared down at his leg suspiciously; the boy unwrapped, stood, said, "Amfatz!" and ran off.

"That's all he says. 'Amfatz!' Everyone expects he's saving himself for something."

"I'd guess 'Amfatz!' means 'Horseshit!' And Norman really is a genius."

"I thought . . . I thought you said you'd changed . . . John?"

"Don't muse me."

Les walked through the room, bearing a tray of assorted juices. When Rhondi tilted her eyes at him, he shifted his feet and pulled his goatee.

"Les? Who have you seen?"

"Well, kid. Ah, not much, you know . . . Mrs. Udall was saying that Charley should have used pig iron instead of copper—ah yeah, 'Pig iron would suggest the somnolent massiveness the theme demands.' That's what she was saying. And let me—oh yeah. That *Times* critic was talking on about abstract programming of automated looms. 'An art which could well be as intimate yet apocalyptic as that of medieval tapestry.' "

"What about my brother?"

"A snerd," Rhondi whispered.

"I couldn't find your brother down there, but the word's to send him up. Well, let's see, kid. There's a Palestine gunrunner. They say he's working Guatemala now. He's in the north corner room, tangling with a pitcher of Manhattans—a big guy, he is. He showed with some sort of sand-and-chalk artist from Peru. And—"

"Thank you, Les." She slid her hand under Leggatt's arm. "Take me to the gunrunner, John?"

"Not tonight."

Smiling upwards, Rhondi pressed her glass into Leggatt's hand and curled his fingers around it. "I understand. Please, keep this for me."

Leggatt watched her slip through the children and press along the wall toward the door. "Understand, Amfatz. You'd better keep your eye on that one, Les."

Les's slate eye narrowed as its brown mate went soft. "There's something about that one, all right."

"A muse." Leggatt rolled her tiny pearl onion along the bottom of her glass. "Another ten years, when she stops talking almost altogether and uses nothing but her eyes—a cup, a vessel. Come pour yourself to me."

"Listen, I like that kid."

"They get to me too, Les."

The blue eye opened, glittering. "There ain't nothing I wouldn't do for that kid, got me?"

"Sure, Les." Leggatt lay his hand on Les's plate of shoulder muscle. "We're in the same corner, you and I."

The blue eye closed. "Yeah. There's nothing I wouldn't do for you either, Johnie. Your friend too." He came up on his toes on the thick carpet that fit the huge nursery as if it had been spooned from wall to wall. "Any time, Johnie. You just call." Scooping the silver tray and holding it over his chest, Les advanced through the children to return below.

⋄ ⋄ ⋄

"So that's your Aztec painter."

Thirty feet below DeFord, Joe Raven stood beside a table covered with sketching paper, his hair combed to his shoulders, twisted body foreshortened and impotent in a dark Italian suit. He seemed to squat while the last of the guests settled with drink and tobacco on the landings punctuating the ascent of the tapered stairway. The low chatter diminished when Raven lifted his face, and the lights extinguished one by one, sending a coil of blackness upwards until the sky seemed to press down. At the bottom of this well in a bright puddle, Raven drew circles of colored chalk in which he fitted fragmented shapes, as if prisoning some jagged metaphysic he found reflected by the stars themselves, for from time to time the dark hollows above his cheekbones would lift toward the sky. As he worked, an atonal humming filled the blackened stairwell, stifling the guests' whispers, and by its rhythmless suck, seeming to flow from everywhere at once. The sound came from within Raven. Becoming a whispered song without language and almost without form, but evidently connected with the stick figures he drew in his circles. DeFord, along with the others, felt himself drawn to the edge of the staircase, but he resisted, leaning against the wall with a start of panic. He could barely make out

Crook, wedged into a tweed jacket, groping along the wall toward the light switches. "So that's your gunrun—" he started to say to Rhondi, when he saw, as the darkness again coiled upwards, Raven's face lift and smile directly into his.

"What's the matter?" Rhondi's hand touched his.

"Get Johnie," he said as the sound from within Raven spiraled, drawing everyone down.

"It-is beauty," Raven whispered, cradling his chalks. "From-earth, from-wind from stars the beau-ty comes to move-these hands. Can-not be called. Must-come." In his fingers the chalks divined the stairway. "Comes-to what must be painted. Comes-down upon him beauty must-be made with these-hands . . ." DeFord watched the chalks swing at him and tremble rigid. Raven writhed, as if to tear loose the aim of his hands. "There in the dark-ness, the beauty is com-ing, filling a-man whose hair-is white, whose limbs-are old but hard . . . There my eyes-see beauty filling him. He stands now-this man." DeFord had stood, his heart beating heavy under his lungs. Whispering began, becoming an excited murmur over which Raven's voice rose in singsong. "Beauty fills him and-must be answered. To-my eyes he glows with-the beau-ty. He moves now. He trying-to deny the-beauty. Pass him to-me. Lead him down-for beauty has blinded him-and he would-fall. Lay your hands and pass-him down."

All DeFord's senses seemed to shrink beneath his lungs, suffocating with the heaviness of hands, whispers, entreaties, until at Raven's table they stole one by one into the puddle of light, echoing his passage downwards:

"Here, let me help you—isn't it exciting?"

Soft hands, passing him down.

"Did he actually see you in the dark?"

"You darling man, so you feel filled with beauty?"

Soft laughter. Whiskey. Perfume.

"Really, isn't it wonderful. Why he's hypnotized us all!"

Something passed over his lap and drew up; he tried to stand but it had tightened, buckling him to the heavy chair. Behind him Proudhomme snickered. DeFord waited, gazing at the needletip of Raven's ice pick slowly circling about him. Raven's singsong came louder and his ice pick scraped faster.

"Beauty-is pain. Pain-death. In this old-man's face-is the beau-ty of death. Asking to be-free. Death and beau-ty are buddies. Budd-dies of this old-man who-runs."

Even as Raven's drill steadied, the darkness brightened, and again and again lights burst in the hallway dome. Confused, the pick withdrew; Crook fumbled at the switches, unable to contain the seepage of light from above. On the landing of the children's rooms, Rhondi stood alone, twisting the dials of a rheostat. With a throttled grunt Raven motioned, and at once Crook responded, one fist a stiffened ball of knuckles and hair, the other swinging at his knee. Guests pressed to the wall as he ascended, face pinched with concentration, and thrust toward Rhondi, who had frozen, hands still shielding the light source. He was halfway when Les stepped from the children's rooms and descended to the narrowest landing. His hands cocked, his body up on his toes, and his head bobbing right and left as the brown eye measured Crook's ascent from one angle, then another. The man's been half blinded, DeFord realized.

Eyes fixed on Rhondi, Crook began his charge. Les did not seem to move at all, simply vanish from the landing and become one with Crook, his hand on the good-eye side a blur from which a dozen sounds, as sharp yet heavy as the reports of a machine pistol, came one with the other. Then Les was back on his landing, and Crook stood shock still, twelve steps below the point of his charge. Slowly his hands explored his face, while his mouth shaped for something. Then a bellowing came from his throat, plunging through scream to rage as he threw himself at the railing and ripped two banisters, only to snap them into sticks. These he flung from him with a howl. His rage steadied, he plucked two heavy ones, and was advancing again when Leggatt called out and started down.

"All right, Joe. Turn off your man. Finish your beauty and pain— Turn him off, Joe." Crook hesitated when Leggatt stepped toward him. "Excuse me." Leggatt went directly to Raven's table, stood by DeFord and poked Raven's chalks. "Well, pain. Yes, pain." He lifted them, squinted, shook his head. "Fairly promising line here—but pain? No. Turn the lights down. Let's all look at this . . . That your assistant?"

"I'm a decorator." Proudhomme sniffled. "Interior decorator."

"Sure you are. Be good enough to dim the lights for us, will you?" Raven nodded, Proudhomme minced, the pit dropped to blackness. Leggatt kept moving, talking steadily. "Let's arrange these in the light. Oh, did I turn it upside—? Well, no matter. Sorry, I see no pain. Does anyone see pain . . . ? No answer."

"I-kill you, Johnie," Raven whispered. "You and the old-man."

"Really, Joe, I can understand how you especially can be obsessed with beauty—but pain? There's none of it here."

The guests stirred, anxious, bored. Raven glared; they silenced.

"They don't understand you, Joe. On the other hand, perhaps they do. Is there pain here?"

Uneasiness, shifting of silks, coughs, whispers.

Raven's ice pick was out and clasped to probe the darkness. "I know-pain."

"Sure you do. By the way, Mr. DeFord here remembers

some fine old logging songs. Perhaps he'll sing us a few."

Approval.

"I-know pain!"

"If someone could furnish a guitar—"

"Pain? Pain?" Raven's face choked black. "You-want pain?" He twisted to the table, ice pick high above the puddle of light. "Stink-ing, fuck-ing pigs! Fuck-king, stink-arg gaah-pi gha—" His fingers splayed down and out as the pick drove deep through his hand into the table.

Silence.

Raven breathed down, a smile whitening his face. "Now." His whisper gathered the darkness. "Now I-paint you-pain . . . here." He daubed the blood of his pinioned hand. "Here is the color-of pain."

"Stop him," a woman cried. "Someone, my God, stop him."

"Here-is the shape-of pain."

Leggatt unbuckled DeFord, whose chest was grunting with a promise of hysteria. "The damn fool." DeFord leaned across at Raven, blood running between them. "You damn fool." He laughed. "That's black cherry. It's set onto that sticker of yours like concrete. You damn fool."

"Take it easy," Leggatt soothed. "Let's get out of here."

"Crook? Get-down here. Crook!" Raven tore at his pick, fingers slippery with blood. "Pigs-fuck-king—" Again and again his free hand dipped up his blood and flung it to the guests. "Want-pain? Here! Fucking pigs. Here-is pain. Here-here-here."

◇ ◇ ◇

Leggatt sat on a kitchen counter, pursing his lips at a gentle steam rising from a saucepan. "Frustrating business —watching water boil."

At a small pantry table DeFord whittled on a cork. "Shouldn't we move on?"

"Give Joe a chance to clear the Village. No doubt he'll hole somewhere to lick his hand." Leggatt poured tea. "What color you prefer? Scotch, bourbon or rye?"

"Light."

Leggatt fished a tea bag. "That's a woman's drink, De-Ford. Now I double-age mine in pure porcelain."

"You took a double age to join the party."

"Our little muse went after Les, not me. I knew nothing until I heard Crook yawping. Ahh. Here she is."

Rhondi bounced in, sat down close to DeFord and stared at the floor. "Are you mad at me, John? Les made me promise I'd always come to him if something happened. Besides, I didn't want you to be hurt." She smiled up to DeFord. "Is that a champagne cork?"

"I wouldn't know. But it's a passable whistle now. For you."

"Will you be able to hear if I signal?"

"When I hear it I'll come."

The kitchen door eased for Les's head, then burst wide to admit his shoulders. He marched to Leggatt. "Dwo un mry, Goni, vre godt to suttel!"

Rhondi giggled. "Oh, Les, you've still your mouthpiece in."

"Vhad?" He thumbed it into his palm and wet his lips. "Johnie? We got to settle. You busted my only action in four months. An—"

"Les? May I see your mouthpiece?"

"What? No, kid, not right now." Les unzipped a pouch and slipped it in.

"You ought to get out of this business, Les."

"Hell. I can't, Johnie. They got all the money. Listen, what the hell you bust my fight for?"

"I expected he would break your head. Why do you store that thing with your tobacco."

"I ain't got a humidor . . . The hell he would have busted me. I was going to take it on the arm, see? So he might bust my arm, so what? Then I was set to give him a rabbit in the throat."

"Is it worth the money?"

"Money? I don't know. Yes, it's worth the money . . . I ought to get out of this business."

"Anyway, how about my friend here? They were going to stick him. And where were you?"

"You mean that little painter that flipped? Jesus. Was he? Hey, I'm sorry."

"I tried to tell you, Les."

"I know, kid. I know. There ain't nothing I wouldn't do for you, you know that. But it didn't seem—I mean—it's hard—you know?"

"You certainly looked good tonight. Ask for a raise."

"Ahh. I don't have to ask, Johnie. They'll give me one automatic . . . So they were going to stick your friend, huh . . . ? I ought to get out of this business."

XII

The air over Washington Square lay heavy yet shallow, for the day had been thick with summer but the night was crisping to fall. And Leggatt, using his teeth to strip rind from a lemon he had pocketed in the brownstone kitchen, chewed its meat, spat its seeds and talked of his life before Elizabeth Street. "Yes. All lots of fun. But then one by one so many of my friends began the chase. At first I found it sort of amusing. Until I saw they all believed it. That is, they had to believe in themselves doing it because they were, after all, doing it. I became quite stupidly outraged. Although as much of it was my sickness—you know—if your friends can't save you, then damn them or change them. Or both. Still, I wasn't very much satisfied with my own work either. Eventually I ended up under the bridge. About as honest a place to start as any."

"And now where?"

Leggatt led onto West Fourteenth toward Christopher. "This where and a few other wheres are the only ones I've found. Then where? You tell me, DeFord. You're the 'where' expert."

Places. Places. In DeFord's memory a thousand intruded, stretching north, receding south, with the pace of a man measuring the sea. "You might say . . . once in a while I get the suspicion I was right out there, pulling for myself, all right. But pulling backwards. So I settled for Oregon."

Leggatt fell into step, studying his feet. "It should be a long time before they beat that where."

"Who? Mr. Nicholas?"

"A where can be eclipsed for years until it forces up some where else. Right now this where is slipping east into Raven's country and north to Harlem. It's not Uncle Nick doing it. It's my brother. Frank falls on wheres like a slumlord on a condemned block. You can follow his work by the respectability mushrooming behind him. Fungus on his string of damp turds."

"It's a handle." Yes, DeFord thought, Leggatt's itch to put handles to everything was very like his own itch to change one town for another, landscape for seascape. Friends you could always keep track of. The crowd he knew were not much for talking anyway, but tended to get together now and then to harvest something—hay, salmon, apples, deer. Their wives had stopped trying to settle him in a long time ago. He himself wasn't sure why they always failed. But it did seem, somehow, no matter how much of a woman they put in front of him, it always came down to his looking at her one day and thinking: Is this what I walked over this country for? Lived all the places I've lived? To settle in and grow old with sweet Mary, handsome Sarah? And about then he would talk of someplace he'd heard or seen, and the clever ones would let the reins slip, might even turn permissive, drawing him deeper into their affections. But after such honeymoons the wandering would seize him tenfold, and he would be possessed with the idea of building something on the Olympic Peninsula, the edge of the desert, the slopes of Mount Hood. And they would joke with him then, seeking to talk it away. Impossible. After a while he would be gone; sweet Mary, handsome Sarah an old friend with whom he exchanged letters until she wrote of her new happiness and he sent the wedding gift.

It was . . . Trying, with the tricks Leggatt's impositions had taught, to sense what he felt about his country, hoping that finally, with the fact of his forced encampment where it had all started, at the very birth of his America, he might find himself—concentrating now on the veritable impossibility of his constant unrest—DeFord struggled with his loneliness, and recalling all the feelings he could possibly and honestly remember, concluded it was merely something about the land being so very vast while its people wanted nothing but to use it up. Given the necessary machinery, they would chew its trees to the stump, quaff its rivers and fill their bellies with its rock and stone, ruminate long into the night, digesting valleys of topsoil, plains of grass. It was . . . No. He could not hang on to it long enough. He just flat had no idea why he did the things he did. Maybe if Leggatt was truly what he called himself, a certified madman, then he was equally insane. Only without the credentials.

"And women, Johnie? What have you done for women?" he asked, aware that three years was a long time, madman or not.

"Oh, I still have some friends. And I met Codgers, and the old monkey was always plotting for me. Arranging things, getting mysterious phone calls, doddering off for two, three days in the middle of an elaborate dinner to research some goddamn theory at the Yale library or the Smithsonian archives. Leaving me slavering, sharing a ten-course Afghanistan wedding feast with a perfectly beautiful little muse."

"Ha!" DeFord remembered a few dinners friends had arranged with a sweet Mary, handsome Sarah. "By the by, I promised him we'd come for breakfast."

"Good. Sunday breakfasts are his favorite. You may get to meet one of his grandchildren. They're all his grandchildren. Christ knows how he manages it."

"What are they like?"

"What Rhondi will grow into. A muse. Girls—they are never women, no matter how old—invariably beautiful with long straight hair and large quiet eyes. They speak barely at all, but then with such softness they arouse all my responsibility to protect innocent things and all my bare-assed lust. Wide sensitive eyes beg you to take and forever protect them from the world, themselves, yourself, everything."

"You mean after three years he's still matching up grandchildren to you?"

"More than ever. Codgers senses I'll be ready to leave the river soon. And he's right. I'm painting well now. Matter of time." Leggatt plucked DeFord by the elbow and maneuvered him to a pile of curbside trash cans. "Until then I prefer to be known as a rather promising but sick young exile." He hefted a can, jerked and pressed, balanced its fifty-odd pounds in his right palm and squatted, leaning left palm on sidewalk and walking a circle with the can straight-armed above his head. "A very sick young man, as you see, DeFord." Leggatt straightened, winked. "I have secrets, DeFord. My strength, for one."

"You had secrets, Johnie." DeFord found a crippled chair and lifted it stiff-armed by its back. Rear legs at right angles to him, he brought the chair to his face, kissing the top of its back and pressing it away. Then he lowered it, and Leggatt tried, successfully except for the kissing part, which he could not manage. DeFord repeated it, with right arm only. I'm an old fool, he thought, feeling his heart quicken. But you have to keep the young studs in line. You were strong. Once.

"I'm damned, DeFord. You're full of surprises."

"I have some secrets too." When you get to my age, he thought, you do your tricks with grip and not with bulk. "We even have a few muses out in my part of the country," he offered, baiting.

Leggatt's eyes narrowed. "Oh?"

"Though we don't call them that. We call them the quiet, handsome types."

They were walking now, together, in stride, through the spangle of Saturday night, Greenwich Village. "Tell me what you have out there, DeFord."

"All right," DeFord said.

◇ ◇ ◇

Turning north on Hudson Street, DeFord quickened to the river smell and talked of the Oregon coast, of what you could still harvest if you had a bit of patience at it. And how the natives back up the little drainages took deer year round, salmon when they spawned, and clams, fish, crab whenever the tide was right. Depending. It all depended. It depended which way you wanted to live. Up drainage a few miles from the sea alone on a dirt road. Or the twenty-thousand-dollar house in town where you sat thigh to flank with your neighbor, and you bought things all the time. But that was something else. He had made his peace with that a long while back. "Where are we headed now, Johnie?"

"Frank should have shown at Rhondi's house. So he's

still at his day's work, I guess. I'm taking us to a bar he owns a good piece of, hoping we'll find him exercising his total recall on the bottle levels. You might find it interesting: since a great poet drank himself to death there it's been very popular. Lesser poets seek his greatness in their glasses, and the money crowd seeks theirs drinking with lesser poets. So you know a place where you could build me a house for practically nothing?"

"Seal Rock, Oregon. There's six miles of accessable drift. Most people use it for stovewood. But if you know what you're after—I could build a tight, roomy little cottage for you and one of your handsome, quiet types for—less than six hundred dollars."

"Six hundred? I don't believe you."

Then be damned. No, I must be tired. DeFord knew his very fatigue was strength, for it allowed him to think of his Raven-spectered future calmly. So he tried to explain what he knew of work and land and people—not much task for a man, more likely a boy and a half, he thought, but it might make the numbness deepen. "Yes, six hundred. Shower, stove, icebox. Course you have to buy the land. Might cost you twice six hundred . . . You don't believe it, Johnie, because you're not thinking of secondhand plumbing, sinks, doors, window frames. You're not thinking of gravity-flow spring water, rock fireplace and miles of driftwood picked over each spring by people looking for sculpture or shingle logs or stovewood or Japanese glass fishing-net floats. But never looking for eave logs nor two-by-eight siding nor drift planks with enough edge left for flooring, nor any of the rest. Because they're mostly like you; they think of how much equipment you need to build a shiny new house or how uphill it is to get a fair buy in an old one. But they don't think of driftwood, junkyards and old-fashioned dump grounds."

"Ye gods! All right! I believe." Leggatt threw his arm

around DeFord. "Listen, you old bastard, what right had you to hike into my life, reeking of optimism, old pine needles and damp wool?" He gestured to and fro over the streets. "Here we approach the bowels of Saturday night, scenes of my last saturnalia, hot with fumes of whiskies, mined with a dozen muses—all the while playing the same old game with my twin. Who is plotting right now with this Kreplun: the sort of harlot with whom I am so incapable of sharing life I receive seventy-six dollars and forty-three cents a month to crawl out of everybody's way . . . Enough."

"I've never seen such a man as you for sorting things."

"Don't question my brain-picking. It will get us a winter stake tonight."

"Does it pay by yard, bushel or hour?"

"By the crock. And stop grinning so. Anyone would think you enjoy this work."

"I've had worse."

"One example."

"Ever repair gut-wagon beds for a slaughterhouse?"

"Ever sell women's shoes at Macy's?"

"Maybe I see what you mean."

At Perry and Hudson, Leggatt made to cross, paused in the gutter and touched DeFord's arm. As a crush of tourists squeezed into a bar a knot of people issued from its side door and packed themselves into a cab. "Too late, damnit."

"There's your brother, getting in by the driver."

The bright yellow car moved into the Village traffic, and Leggatt put his hands in his rear pockets, pursing his lips. "Well, I tried. The hell with it now."

"There's one more place we might find your brother."

"Eddie's bar. Bert's old place. Yes, damn you. You might have forgotten it. Yes, Frank may be there. He seems to be making fast rounds tonight, gathering up the week's loot. Now if you'd taken that job of Bert's and we had Eddie's shirt with us, we'd be ahead by five bucks."

"I don't need his money. Besides, I have you. You got me back my check; now I'll help you get—"

"Okay. Okay. Christ, DeFord, but you're the stubbornest son of a bitch—" They crossed Hudson, walked Perry to the river and retraced south. "Didn't take you a moment to spot Frank. How?"

"Why, he's a grain match for you."

"The hell he is. Mustache, forty pounds heavier, three-hundred-dollar suit."

"I met you first."

"You may have something. Frank was the first-born, you know. Slipped in fat and sassy. I came along three hours later under duress—forceps and all—backwards."

"Tell me about your family."

"Mother was forty-seven when we were born, and died at fifty-five, so I don't remember a hell of a lot, except that she occasionally confused us. It seemed to me from our beginnings, John was myself, and Frank Frank. But now and then I remember catching mother off guard, with a look of delighted confusion. Neither she nor my father expected us; I don't think he ever really got over it, although he very much tried. He was older than she and died a few years after her—seems he had run off to the Great War, been gassed, and his chest never fully mended. Anyway, he died when we were ten, so Frank and I lived with uncles and aunts—all of them quite old, very loving. At sixteen we were sent to the family lawyer, who was then—by God—in his nineties, I swear." Leggatt laughed, a short bark of amusement. "We had come into a legacy of eight thousand apiece, provided we used part or all at a university. As the old lawyer explained, my father never saw the need for universities, although he was proud his country possessed them. But toward the end, he became very unsure and worried for us. So he decided we would be best off at a college, in the hands of professional educators. I remember that old fellow pushing up from his roll-top desk, shuffling over and saying goodbye in a And-may-God-have-mercy-on-your-soul singsong . . . I've had seven years with the books—with a year off for Korea when the Army commissioned me for godknowswhy—and seven years outside."

"You're thirty-five?"

Leggatt laughed. "You mean I don't look it. Well, I don't feel it. Usually I feel a hundred and forty-seven, but then I remember Codgers and realize I'm indulging myself. So I settle for a rather down and dirty fifty-eight. Right now I'm slipping back toward seventeen—babbling about myself because I've let you prod me after Frank. Because I made the good try and all that."

"We'll stay with it. Almost whipped now."

Leggatt shrugged and pushed open the door to Eddie and Bert's Fo'c'sle Bar and Restaurant.

◇ ◇ ◇

"Eddie? No, he sold out his share too." Frank Leggatt's bartender carefully rolled a straight pin between teeth and tongue, studying them. "Guess he couldn't take some of the new policies."

"Actually, we're looking for Frank." The bartender clamped lips and busied himself with two pitchers of beer. Leggatt fingered a few pickled beans in a bowl. "Tell you what. I'll show you how to fill this place with real paying tourists. Deal?"

"Sure. I get rid of those damn pickled beans. The tourists know they're Out with the In crowd and won't come near the bar so long as they're here." Toting pitchers, he disappeared into a back room.

"Well, I'll be damned."

"Your brother likes those beans or he doesn't like money or both," DeFord said.

Leggatt swung from the bar, peered into the back room and returned. "Packed with the crowd Frank just raided. But no Frank. That explains the beans. Discourage the tourists, keep the place cozy for Frank's In crowd. Until they're coming here regularly, have worked up a tab. Then let the word out, clean up on tourists, and always have another bar ready for the In crowd when they get tired of being stared at."

The bartender returned, laid the cash drawer on the bar and searched the till for something. Leggatt studied the thin piles of money. "Did Frank just leave?" The bartender's pin clamped. "I'm John Leggatt, his brother."

The pin loosened, the bartender dealt a card onto the wood. "Why didn't you say, for crissake? Yeah, now I see the resemblance. Frank dropped by, made a phone call and had to move out fast. He wants you to follow right away. Here's the address. His driver's looking for you—went back to Frank's other place."

"One Wall Street," Leggatt read. "One Wall Street? Wall Street? Let's get out of here, DeFord. Let's—"

"Get your money, mend the lock on my room and rest up."

Leggatt prodded the card. "Someday—"

"That's fair. You might make wages in the Oregon brush and never seem out of place. But you were saying . . . ?"

Leggatt cleaned his fingernails with his brother's card. "Well, this is what I wasn't swearing about: Frank has bought this bar and raided the drawing people from his other bar so he can coax in the money crowd when he's sold his other interests. I wasn't swearing that, even though I happen to like his partners, who will have a shallow pot when Frank is done. No, I wasn't swearing that. Although once I might, I haven't time for it any more. I was swearing over the way he's sucked me into it—and I promise, he'll have you in somehow before daylight. But you don't believe, do you?"

"No."

"You know there's something about you, DeFord. If you were a lot younger, I'd want to kick the shit out of you. But it will suffice to let it run. I've taken a lot of crap lately; I hope you have at one time or another."

"I've had my share."

The bartender grinned. "So you're Frank's brother? I'll be damned. What you want? On the house."

"DeFord, did I say no whiskey until the job was over?"

"You said it."

"Afraid of that. Black coffee, then."

"Two," said DeFord.

"Let mine cool while I pick up Frank's car."

DeFord tried not to think and was having fair luck when Tanner made his way heavily from the street. "Hello, neighbor. Saw Johnie leaving. Thought I'd—"

"You were to stay in your room."

"Listen," the bartender explained. "Your buddy here's got to move on. Frank's orders. Tourist bait like your friend here—"

"Give him some coffee."

"He's got to move on."

"Coffee."

The bartender slid whiskey to Tanner. "Here. Have some fun before you go. No hard feelings."

"Going to help me back, DeFord?" Tanner's hands came around his glass.

"I've a job to finish. In the morning—"

"Rest"—Tanner's hands lifted his glass—"my case."

"Want a chaser?" asked the bartender.

"Going for one now."

"Hear me. You go back to your room. In the morn—"

"Yessir." Tanner focused onto DeFord. "There must be something good for you, neighbor. There must be something good for everyone."

DeFord watched him lurch to the street. "Ever skin a bobcat?" his mouth said, thinking even as he said it, I have made a mistake. I will regret this.

The bartender plucked the pin from his mouth. "Not yet."

"Well," DeFord explained into his coffee, "there's only one way to do it. No matter what people tell you there's only one way to skin a cat."

"If you say."

"It's true. But don't believe it. It should not be true, so don't believe it."

◇ ◇ ◇

All the long way through the darkening streets DeFord sat in a corner of Frank Leggatt's Mercedes-Benz, watching the city's glitter fade as the car moved south toward the great silent skyscrapers of the financial district. It would be daylight in a few hours, and surely all would be over soon. While Leggatt chatted with his brother's chauffeur, the car, with its odor of leather and rosewood, its heavy moving silence seemed more and more a promise.

"Did you hear?" Leggatt muttered, easing into the cushions. "I'm to exhibit again in the spring with Kreplun. Even Frank's driver knows. An old friend. He's very happy for me."

"I'm sorry, I wasn't paying attention."

"Doesn't matter. After Elizabeth Street, I guess I should be good for something. Even as simple a thing as being dangled as a sort of arty collateral when Frank sells his other bar in order to buy into a gallery in order to exhibit

Kreplun in order to clinch next year's hundred thousand."

"You'll get your winter stake out of it."

"Exactly. You know, I'm a bit sorry I said . . . about kicking you out."

"I've called you extravagant many times."

"Three."

"Three extravagants cancel one shit-kicking."

"Done."

Frank's limousine delivered them to the huge bank, where a tipsy elevator girl explained that she had been instructed to deliver them first to a private office. As they entered the suite of rooms too well furnished to be an office, DeFord, his heart full of promise that the long night would soon be over, followed Johnie toward the sound of splashing water.

"Come-in, John-nie, the water's fine." Joe Raven floated naked in a tub, his upper body heavily muscled, his broken shanks squiggling underwater like snakes. "Crook? Lock-the-door, please, while we have-a-talk."

"You-must take good care of-yourself, old man." With an oval of mint-colored soap, Raven lathered his chest, and reached to the golden-tiled floor for whiskey. "You need some-kind of-insurance. Some-thing you-can trust." He held his glass for Crook to pour fresh, then called to Proudhomme, who was looting the adjoining room. "Got-it yet, Al-fred?" Proudhomme fetched a first-aid kit and cut Raven's bandages. "See how good he-is with Crook's knife? Al-fred would have-made a wonderful surgeon."

"Ugghs," Proudhomme lisped as Raven examined the purplish entrance and exit of his wound.

"But Al-fred was too-sensitive. Crook here, he is almost-as-good and might have been a fine-butcher, but he was . . . how shall I-say . . . too impatient. Crook?"

"Not with cats, Joe."

"Crook is very-patient with cats."

Leggatt ran water over his cigarette and fed its sodden butt to the golden sink-throat. "Joe, you've got a nice thing going here, but we're rather in a hurry, so if you don't mind—"

"So-soon, Johnie? Leaving so-soon?" Crook plucked his knife from Proudhomme, but Raven waved it away. "Anytime you-want, Johnie. I was hoping we-would have a talk first." He withdrew his ice pick from the suds out of which his body rose, shiny as wet teak. "There was a-time I came close to punching this into the old-man's ear." His pick punched to its ball through the mint soap, forcing a squiggle of jelly onto his hand. This Raven held, and pointing the grayish knots of his cheeks at Leggatt, he sniffed. "Like-money, John-nie."

"Don't see how you can tell. This room reeks of barge bilge. When did you last have a bath, Joe?"

"When-was the last time any-one had a bath, John-nie?"

"I swim every morning. You should try the river."

"I would-not swim the river any-more, John-nie. I've seen sharks many-times. You have to watch hard, but you-can see them." He adjusted the soap to cover his pick, then lathered his back. "Once I saw two-big sharks tear-up a body once. Did-not take them very-long. No joke, John-nie. They come in from east of Long-Island. You've read it. Well, they-are up into the-river too."

"That will take a lot of joy from my morning swims."

"Any-thing for a friend. But as I-was saying, John-nie. Before you go I-want to say I-have changed my mind about the old-man here. Ahhhhh, but-you are leaving. And we-have not even begun to-talk."

Leggatt moved toward the door with DeFord. "Sorry, Joe. Some other time. I wouldn't want to push your hospitality."

"It-is not just hosp-pital-lity. It is something I learned just-now from your brother."

Leggatt returned to the bathside. "My brother?"

"My, you certainly are-curious. I re-marked to Frank how curious you-were. And you-know what? He said you-had always been curious." Raven grinned terribly. "Have you always been so-curious?"

Fool, DeFord thought. Damn, damn fool. The fear of Raven came in spasms, but at the instant he wanted to surrender to laughter, he sensed the hysteria beyond it; as Raven seemed not to belong to his life at all, he made no appeal. It was at once unbelievable yet perfectly acceptable. He returned to his seat in the gilted bath, knowing it was the worst possible choice, but he was so furious with Leggatt's extravagant curiosity that he was willing to punish himself, destroy himself as proof at last that Leggatt was utterly impossible. Quite beyond thinking, he watched Raven lift twisted lower limbs to scrub.

"So you-swim every morning, John-nie? I used to swim all the time. On-the reservation."

"A healthy fun-loving Mohawk—"

"On-on-daga."

"—Onondaga boy come to the big city to seek his fortune. Now what's this about my brother?"

"Your-brother and Mr. Kreplun had-left the Washington-Square party be-fore I met the old-man there. You know something, John-nie?" He extended his bandaged hand. "I'm glad this-happened."

"Your lecture on beauty change your life, Joe?"

"No-thing changes, John-nie. But your brother met me before-it happened. When he-and Mr. Kreplum came back-to find you, we met again on the-street. We had a-long talk about art-and-things, and then it was too late for him to-look for you. So he asked if I would come to talk about art-and-things to some of his-friends. I suggested he-send his-car back for-you so we would all be-to-gether at last."

"So now you are bathing for the party, where we'll all discuss art and money with Frank's friends."

"But first I-wanted to clear up our-business. And-to apologize."

"This is the inspirational part: my brother's influence."

Raven dressed, pausing to sip whiskey. "You make it-very difficult, but I deserve it I-know. Talking to your-brother, I-learned you have to-offer something, John-nie. So I asked Joe what you-have to offer that old-man who's always running? What would-you offer John-nie, who could-be your buddy but re-fused because you-were too greedy?" He sat at a red kidney desk, a million or two city lights glittering beyond him. "And I thought: insurance. One-day John-nie is going to be very famous with his ex-hibi-tion and all. But until, he has-to winter Bowery. Now if all-those men are to help John-nie's brother buy a gallery so John-nie can exhibit and become famous, then it-is time for me to help too. I-felt very humble, John-nie."

"Protection."

"Soon you-will have to go back to Elizabeth Street. Nothing changes, John-nie. Any-thing could happen to you or your buddy this win-ter."

"All right." Leggatt held his hand to DeFord. "Give me your check . . . Now, Joe, this is a bank, right? So find us a book of blank checks . . . Now, DeFord, sign your check here."

"No." Even as he said it, DeFord knew he would, for Raven's face distorted to a smile. He reached for the pen.

"Never mind," said Leggatt. He signed it himself: "For deposit only—Lyle DeFord."

"That-is not his-signature! Crook!"

"For crissake—it makes no difference." Leggatt opened a book of checks. "How about twenty-five a month, Joe?"

The ice pick steadied. "I kill-you now, Johnie. You and the old-man."

"What the hell for? The signature on these will be the same as on DeFord's check. But these will be made out in advance. Each month you'll be able to cash one for twenty-five."

"Apiece."

"Insures both of us?"

Raven's ice pick disappeared into his sleeve.

"All right. Here's three checks for the next three months."

"The de-posit is only for one twenty-five."

"They'll be another pension check next month."

"Fill-out the whole book."

"I may leave Elizabeth Street by then."

Raven sipped whiskey. "You-will never leave, John-nie. Not with-out me."

"Okay. I'll fill the book."

"No. Just sign-them. After your exhibit we will readjust payments."

Leggatt flapped the checks under Raven's nose. "For crissake, I can't fill lines with signatures. These are legal documents for the fattest bank in the city. Not a goddamn Monopoly game."

"I'll cash the first-Monday afternoon."

"I'll deposit by then." Leggatt pocketed DeFord's pension check, and they left Raven rocking uneasily over his whiskey.

I should be grateful, DeFord thought. The money will hold him awhile. Their elevator sank safely toward the party below. I have my place, he thought to console himself—it deepened his disgrace. Naked. Naked. No. NO. "Here!" He seized a match and scraped its head to flame. "Give me my check. He'll have none of it."

"Damn you, DeFord. You're your own worst friend. I

said I'd deposit it, didn't I? Monday we will. We'll have Codgers cash it for us somewhere. Joe will be stuck with a book of paper and— Careful, you'll burn your fingers."

DeFord let the flame creep to his flesh before pinching it out. There, he thought, feeling the justice of the pain. That will teach you to keep your mouth tight.

◇ ◇ ◇

Kreplun found them as they stepped off the elevator into the party. He led them to a bar, where Leggatt reached for whiskey, sighed, took coffee instead, and DeFord watched two Staten Island ferries glimmer toward each other, become a gaudy collision of light, then struggle apart. He had magnificent news. Did either of them realize that at this very instant Johnie's brother was working out specifications for the new gallery in which he, Kreplun, and Johnie would exhibit this spring? A moment ago Frank had left with one of the bank men. For where? They could never guess. The roof. Yes, what a genius Johnie's brother. There on the very top—the city below, lights winking a trillion golden dollars—there Frank would plead for the ultimate investment, the commitment of money to art, the fulfilling service of a great lending house to the greatest of cities. If he, Kreplun, had but one half Frank's intuition he would be a great, great artist.

Kreplun flowed on, his words smelling of bourbon and toothpaste while one hand roamed his upper lip as if to pick his nose. But he sought only his mustache, a thin harassed strip the color of pigs' eyelashes. Of course, he was saying, had it not been for that Aztec painter Franklin might have had a more difficult time with the banking men. But there Raven had come, with such a magnificent face, such a powerful deformity. Raven had spoken hardly a word, but what feeling, what—

"Sorry." Leggatt laid down his cup. "You'll have to excuse us." Kreplun understood. It was the excitement. The late hour. Great news affected people quite—

Leggatt guided DeFord between conversations until they gained the hallway, sprang to an empty elevator, and the doors scissored. "Ahh . . . Would you mind if I tried again to see Frank?"

"Was Joe in the room with us?"

"Yes. With Crook drunk but in tow. I hoped our short-change nonsense would hold till Monday . . . It is Frank I want to see."

"I know. I know."

"I'm sorry. You're tired. The hell with it. Let's get some rest." He punched first floor and they plummetted.

"No. We agreed to look for a job for me or return my check and find your brother."

"Getting your check is a damn good half of it."

"I'm thinking of tomorrow, when we realize we're but damn good half done."

Leggatt's finger stabbed again, and their descent eased upon the seventh floor. "I suppose you're right. Besides, we're better off resting on the roof than trying to make the subway with old mangled groin prowling the streets. Just to be safe, we'll go back up in a service elevator."

They found one at the farthest end of a corridor where old women were cleaning offices and a room of machines still clacked and sorted the week's business under the supervision of two electronic eyes and an automatic sprinkler.

The roof was half the breadth of a quarter section, DeFord guessed—scattered with corrugated sheds housing ventilation and conditioning outlets. Eighty acres of fenced pebbles traversed with interlocking open tiles. Irrigation? Now what wildcat crop would they grow up here? DeFord was ready to believe anything. Had a tractor appeared hauling cultivator, fertilizer box and a forty-foot wheat drill, he would have believed. The moon was high, casting buildings in ivory gray as soft as moleskin, while the shadowed places seemed bottomless at their blackness. Here and there people moved, taking the air with whiskey and cigarettes.

"Watch your step over these drains," said Leggatt.

Of course, not ditches. Drains. "I had best get some rest. Perhaps one of those sheds is open."

"We'll find one before I look for Frank. But first come to the edge."

At the railing he realized the immensity of the city, the boundlessness of its stone and concrete and glass. Nine millions. More yet; two hundred millions feed it. And beyond the oceans, millions more. Half the paper in the world received its magic from the concrete acres below. "I would like to sleep now."

"Of course. Sorry." Under an immense steel obelisk they found a shed open, a light burning at a desk, walls lined with electronic gauges. Leggatt lay new sheets over a corner cot and gestured DeFord to lie down.

"Someone works here." Perhaps they would not mind were he to lie on the floor, though.

"Use the cot. I'll talk to whoever works here and get us straight."

He lay down, and Leggatt's words receded to nothing, so quickly did his body sink to sleep.

◇ ◇ ◇

DeFord dreamed: the Henry Mountains of Utah, early spring on the seat box of Simpson's wagon, a heavy Winchester between his knees. Simpson's hounds, scrabbling the wagon bed to scent the melting snowfield. The hounds were Bull, half pitbull (for grit, Simpson explained), half redbone (for nose), the bitch Gin (all redbone, all nose—too much nose to stay long at tree), and their pups, Durham (for voice) and Sloe. ("For the flat hell of it, I'm tired of shooting pups what don't prove, so we'll let her run another season and see if she takes.") DeFord had come upon Simpson in early fall—1930 or '31—where the old man crouched by a roadside, scoring a new Winchester and swearing. "You trying to slip up on me? . . . No, you ain't disturbing. Can't make this thing hit the moon broadside. Shoot much yourself? . . . Good. Then try it. I'll learn you." Two hours later Simpson squatted contentedly, lifting his peasant's face at DeFord, its almost perfect cherub's mouth puckering over a lower lip packed with snuff. "You working now? . . . Still a long cut better them college men jumping windows back East. My eyes is going, though. Couldn't hit my ass with both hands and a hat . . . I'll be honest—give you a quarter what the dogs hold long enough for you to kill. But mind you gone to do it my way."

Then what was it he feared? Simpson's way was no more demanding than any job he had put himself to. Surprising perhaps, almost awesomely effective. Pledged to its secrets, DeFord had kept his word. When the other hunters plied him with beer they could not afford he sensed they were swarming him, but he was no longer so green as to mistake their hunting for sport rather than the only means remaining to bring in food and tobacco. Neither was he so green as to feel seven feet tall when Simpson tallied their winter kill: twenty cougar, sixty bobcat, eighteen lynx, fifteen bear. Sixteen hundred dollars of meat, bounty, and hides—as much as the entire town saw that season, DeFord's share more than anyone in the town would match in a year. When his town was flat broke, Simpson had stepped from a shakeboard shack and salvaged its pride, placing its name in all the sporting magazines, twice in the Boone and Crockett listings. Simpson —his town's joke, its expected and accepted madman, tolerated not even as he was enough white to be neither Indian nor nigger, tolerated only as his town already possessed its drunk, its rich man, and its failure, it made room for a man raising litter after litter of hounds, shooting one after another when they did not measure up to his standard. DeFord merely carried the guns and used them in Simpson's way.

Then what was it he feared? He had never been so green as to congratulate himself for keeping the old man's secrets of killing, nor had he felt more than a hired instrument in taking eighty-six hundred pounds of bear, cougar, and cat without losing a dog. And he had respected Simpson's obsession to prove that when everything else had failed his town, he, Simpson could save its pride, if only for three winters, or one—until agriculture and commerce and trade worked again and hunting became what it was meant to be: a tradition, a sport, a pastime. This obsession DeFord respected even above the secret of killing, but even more he respected the old man's knowledge of cat crossings, game trails, storm-by-storm, moon-by-moon wanderings of deer and bear, prediction of weather, forage, and atop all—a flawless anticipation of the plundering of predators among the nomadic herds. Yes, DeFord respected Simpson's madness even more than his success.

He only feared he would fail the old man.

He had not failed, even though he had forgotten to pack the small rifle and so the killing had violated Simpson's method and could have lost all the hounds. For Simpson never used his guns for sport; sport was the running. Shooting was simply an act of dispatching so perfectly the game fell lifeless. For this Simpson trained DeFord to detach himself completely from the fever of the run, to stand apart from those primal memories which each and every time rose to possess him. This other hunters had not learned: no man, whoever he be, could keep his nerves completely when walking up to cornered game. Some instinct warred against it, rising strong as sex, quick as fear. But with DeFord, the forced detachment became as effective as it ever could—unless, DeFord said once to his teacher, unless a man were a machine.

"If he ain't got no soul," Simpson replied. "If he ain't got no soul, you mean. Then maybe he could flat feel nothing and plain kill something as beautiful and vicious as them cats. Or as hard to believe as them cougar. 'Cause that's it, ain't so? A man can tromp this brush thirty years, maybe never cross cat or cougar. Never once. He sees where cats jump young does, claw their eyes, then eat slow, or where the cougar he slips into a deeryard and feeds every two days, till spring they's nothing but a bunch half-ate carcasses and the drifts full of starved young where they snow-drowned when they just couldn't take no more smell of cougar and blood. Oh, a man maybe sees lots of that. But he never sees the thing what's made it. By and by he goes to running the critters, and one day it's there up a tree, looking at him—the thing what he knows the woods are full of but he never seen. You look up there and it's as big as a crazy woman, and if it looks at you God help your hounds, 'cause sooner or later a real big one's gone to be where you knew damn well he'd be but you didn't believe till you saw him, which you can't ever believe till each time you see him again—just like the first. Well, someday a real skookum will look back at you, and you'll know if you don't kill it you'll never be able to walk the brush again, or walk anywhere at night, because now it seen you it knows what you are. It knows all makes you any different from anything it kills and eats is a hundred pounds of noisy dogs and a Winchester. Oh, I seen it too much. Felt it too much. Right then you stop killing. You freeze and flat shoot, that's all—just pull trigger. And that nothing-but-kill-and-eat devil of a thing comes piling out, bad-gutted or maybe only his little toe shot off, and your hounds pile on. That's what some call sport, but not me. You got to have dogs to keep alive. And you ain't having dogs long, making sport of killing. That's what I mean about soul. If a man had no soul, he could kill perfect each time. But the only thing what got no soul is up there in front of the gun. A man now, he got to be trained like you been trained; he got to have a training like what I trained you. And he got to remember. Even then he's going to fuck up sooner or later. You're going to fuck up sooner or later, Lyle. I hope to God I ain't under the tree when you do." All this Simpson said while their horses scrabbled higher into the timber. Then he reined up and turned in his saddle to look straight at DeFord. "But the hell, that's what you got dogs for too. So when it happens, don't let it worry you none. But if it happens a next time, you best go down the road and find yourself another line of work."

It had not happened. Even the day DeFord forgot the small rifle, they had not lost a dog. But it had taken too much out of him and that spring he went on farther west. He liked old Simpson, liked him a lot. But the killing took too much from him.

It seemed a simple thing. With Simpson coaching, he took lynx and bobcat low in the brisket, where their hearts lay within an inch of fur and the small bullet did not knock them down, but bled them out until they tumbled lifeless. Bear he took with the heavy Winchester in the lungs, and they drowned fast. Most hunters heart-shot bear—which left a lot of time for terrible mischief among the dogs—or head-shot them, which was almost worse, for like any pig, bear could thrash a full minute with half their brains gone. With cougar he used the little gun—a trick that seemed to defy all logic. But a paunch-shot cougar would lie blinking until he bled to death inside. It was a simple thing, but DeFord felt less of a man because of it, especially with the cougar. Yet he knew the only other shot was with the Winchester just forward and a thumb's breadth below the ear—too dangerous. Besides, he too had seen the ravaged deeryards, and that helped.

The day of his dream he had forgotten the little gun. But they were high above deer, as Simpson suspected the bear were digging out early—fasted lean and sweet of meat. They were surprised to cross signs of lynx: round, even pads in a purposeful line straight down drainage. "Must have tired of doe meat and made an early circle high to pick off some snowshoes. Same difference, but I wish you hadn't of forgot the twenty-two," Simpson said. The dogs went to work, shuttling red and whining through the snowy brush. "They'll have a time warming him—ice crystals in his tracks. Made just after midnight. Still, there's five dollars sleeping up a tree with a bellyful of rabbit I'd guess. That Winchester will get us bounty even if it messes the hide." The dogs returned, angry but working hard. "Hunt 'em up!" Simpson shouted. "HUNT 'EM UP!" Then Bull and Gin and finally the pups settled, and just beyond sight broke into sharp frantic howls, pounding the small canyon as they turned down drainage, milled, backtracked, and lined out going high. "Must have caught him lying up under a windfall. Jesus, they've got a hot one. Figured we'd be sitting—Christ! Listen!" The hounds bayed frantically. "Pile out! That ain't no cat. They jumped track onto something big!"

A green brassy taste rising on his tongue, DeFord waded drifts straight for the roar of the dogs until the old man threw up his hand and whirled, eyes filled with white. At his feet, fully six inches across, lay tracks of a cougar beside which the hound prints seemed impossibly frail, not merely insignificant but veritably obscene in their presumption. And yet, and yet a half mile farther up ridge the furious mindless sound did not abate. My God, DeFord thought. They've treed that thing!

"I don't see how they'll hold," Simpson yelled, plunging ahead, "unless he's gone up to see what it's all about. When he figures who's top dog, he'll pile out on him. Catch old Gin too. And with them pups we'd might as well be after him with switches."

His memory darkened and it was himself peering into the shadows, with whom? Leggatt? Yes, Leggatt behind, negligently carrying the rifle. He whirled to urge Leggatt forward, and Simpson's cry escaped his throat: "Hurry! Jesus, hurry!" But Leggatt seemed committed to other things, oblivious to the vortex of unintelligible sound pleading, threatening, drawing them to its deafening purpose. Its promise pulled DeFord through the brush, its clamor possessing his senses as if he were animal itself, leaping to throw hands, teeth, feet upon everything bestial and soulless and wild. "Take him!" Simpson screamed. "Take him, DeFord!" He was under the tree now, among the furious, hysterical, blind hound-bellowing, the thing on a branch directly above, three hundred pounds of cat—the biggest, he'd have to be the biggest ever seen—he looked eleven feet long, kicking and swearing and screaming the hounds back, while Leggatt—no, it was DeFord—while DeFord, himself, but behind him now as well, lifted the Winchester ever so slowly and steadied it on a tree, and he Simpson-DeFord was tearing at the leash wrapped around his middle, grabbing for Bull, an outrageous machine of noise under the cougar, who caught Bull and dragged him back, yelling, "Take him! Take him, Johnie!" And Bull was Sheriff as Raven leered down, hands bristling with ice picks, stretching to him, while Leggatt just stood there and pointed the Winchester, and he yelled, "Take him! Kill him. Kill! Kill! Kill!"

XIII

"Mother needs you
Mother wants you
come back to Mo-ther and
Jesus"

sings the Salvation Army foursome on their Sunday corner, while Dee Bee Smith—suited, bathed, shampooed, shaved, stomach growling fiercely for muscatel and bottom itching just enough to keep his back ramrod-straight—awaits the Respectables' long black car and receipt of the package They would have him deliver. Almost sober for the first time in eighteen years, Dee Bee's body is numbed, and somewhat confused and humiliated by the initial shock of its withdrawal from wine. The unbelievable success of disguise promises escape will be childishly easy; he has only to convince Them he will deliver their package, thereby accepting responsibility. Disguise, therefore, has two purposes: it indicates he has already joined their forces, and it will allow enough confusion among any more of Them roaming the block to expedite escape. He has only to ditch Pearshape, which will be especially easy if he takes the package to the old lumberjack—a thing he should do anyway, for had not Johnie's friend brought the fiver, plan would be impossible.

"Would you give something to help the unfortunate Bowery man, sir?"

"Memo," answers Dee Bee, manic now with the beauty of plan. "Memo: Each man is his own religion."

Of course, Dee Bee thinks, Mother! He remembers the first months on block: how important never—no, never—to mention Mother. Wives, children, anyone—never Mother. With an Elizabeth Street man, memories of Mother can part the headiest curtains of wine to plant the seeds of remorse and guilt. This was difficult for Dee Bee to learn, for unlike many, he had been a Respectable for a long time, and his Mother always so Respectable that the day she had finally been committed to an insane asylum, Dee Bee had been transfigured with the logic of the act. It was exactly where she belonged, and he had known that sooner or later all her friends, sisters and daughters would join her there behind the broken-glass walls. It was more than the end of the world for his mother; she had been fulfilled, used, reclaimed.

Yet other block people are not so fortunate, and Dee Bee recognizes in the Salvation Army songs the horror of their Sunday work. Even bass-drum girl, so pretty and gallant, is a monster of righteousness. They give no quarter in their passion to reclaim. For respectability. A wino here, a rubbydub there. But no matter. Evil is everywhere. Yet.

"Memo:
To: All branches
From: Dee Bee Smith, Elizabeth Street

All our mothers—"

Careful! Danger!

The great automobile has turned onto block, and walking beside it is the young man in the rich gray coat. Now it nuzzles the curb, the young man coming alone, in his right hand a rolled newspaper. No danger, Dee Bee promises, looking quickly at his hands and pretending to straighten his tie. No, hands are not shaking. He moves to the stairwell, where Pearshape has told him to stand, and takes from his pocket the broken cigarette, as Pearshape instructed; hands are yet steady as he raises his eyes to ask for a match. Ramrod straight, nerves in his legs firing wildly, he stares at the handsome young man and sees behind the college-boy eyes fear and death and murder and blood.

"La tua . . . ah . . . sigaretta é rotta, é tu voi accenderla?"

Dee Bee hears nothing. Deep within him he is thinking: Of course there is blood and killing in this one's eyes. He is one of Them, isn't he? They start early, Respectables do.

"Ho detto che la tua sigaretta é rotta."

What is this? He speaks to me in a foreign tongue? "Memo: Dee Bee Smith is one-hundred-percent American. And . . . and . . ." He gropes with Pearshape's instructions. "Oh. And yes, I would like a . . . match for my cigarette . . . but I don't smoke."

The young man wets his lips. He thumps his rolled newspaper, smiling. "So not everyone in this town speaks his goddamn language?" He grins as if it were a thing they might share, but all the while his eyes fasten to stoops, doorways, windows, alleys. "Well"—the newspaper roll tips as College Boy straightens, and a long package pitches into a garbage can below—"there will be a policeman along in four minutes the latest. You'd better hurry."

Feigning reluctance to depart, he slaps Dee Bee's shoulder, then strolls away as Dee Bee feels the shaking in his knees anew. Careful! Danger!

The long black car slips soundlessly past, a face appears to mark his forever. Gray gloves flick and the limousine corners after its college boy. Dee Bee sinks to the stoop and fumbles for his square of silk. His mouth is making little noises, and his body aches for wine. "Memo:— Memo:—" But nothing comes. He sips from his pint, and gradually his panic ebbs, leaving him exhausted, enervated. I'll never make it. Never should have tried . . . the memory of their faces marking him for eternity—ahhh —they were truly Respectables, those two . . . heh heh. I will escape them.

Across Elizabeth, Pearshape—grinning from ear to ear, the tic under his eye writhing as if that slit had been packed with salt—bolts from an alleyway, then scuttles back as a police car corners onto the block, then another and another, all the while Dee Bee is moving down the stairwell to pick up the sausage-shaped package.

Rather heavy, Dee Bee thinks, and jamming forty thousand dollars' worth of uncut heroin under his arm, he strolls toward DeFord's apartment, oblivious of everything but the memo forming in the back of his head. "Memo," he says, relinquishing it. "Memo: All our mothers belong behind broken-glass walls."

◇ ◇ ◇

"What's the matter?" drawled Leggatt, sitting on the cot and offering coffee. "Bad dream?"

The sun lacked but minutes to rise—DeFord could sense its heat even before he turned to the window of the workshed. "No . . ." I don't want to kill anyone, he thought. God knows. "Yes."

"My friend"—Leggatt nodded at a smallish man in

work clothes, bent over a hot plate—"is making a fresh pot. Have a swallow and then tell me whom I am to kill."

"It was . . . a dream. Thank you. A cougar, mountain lion." He sipped and the dread of it ebbed, but his hand still shook. "I once killed . . . a large one." He felt better, talking it away. "For a man named Simpson. Point of fact, it held the record almost ten years. Then someone . . . I heard . . . topped it in British Columbia."

"Really? I'd never thought you were a hunter."

"I'm not. I wasn't. I did the shooting part. It was . . . a job. We never lost a dog."

"I'm damned. You're full of surprises. Was it a bad time? The big one?"

"No." The workman straightened from his coffee makings, smiled and busied himself as DeFord finished his coffee and tallied his now steady hands. "That is, the shot was not easy. And the old man—Simpson—I do believe he expected I was not going to back him. You see, I was only an instrument . . . it was agreed from the start, and Simpson felt things I wasn't given leave to feel." He filled his lungs. "No matter. I had not thought of it for a long time."

DeFord sipped coffee, refreshed now and surprisingly unconcerned. "But you and I, we finished our work, didn't we?"

"No." Leggatt drained his cup and pitched its dregs into the sun.

"My brother closed his gallery deal before I could get to him. So let's have breakfast with Codgers and then fix the lock on your door."

At the roof edge Leggatt touched DeFord's arm. "How do you feel?"

He breathed air fresh from the sea. "Ready to go."

DeFord felt swollen with energy and the sort of spunk that brings a man to his feet. He paused, sensing memories. For he knew and loved each part of his country to which the sun brought light but half a day. He knew and loved the mountains of the West, and his country's shores, valleys, plains. And he thought of his land as an endless thing—so colossal and varied that any single judgment, any one statement about its people or the way it acted upon its people, was futile. No matter how men tried to match their neighbors, no matter what millions spoke alike, heard alike, watched alike, they would never force upon their land a single way of being. That he, or Leggatt, or even Codgers could explain his country, those forces working upon a man who might choose to live in Arizona, Montana or Louisiana or Alaska or Maryland, was absurd. There would always be some damn mountain man or swamp man or desert man offering something right from the mountain or swamp or desert itself. The people could be damned, he thought. The people be damned. The people are damned—no difference. Their country is too goddamned big.

"Careful," said Leggatt. "You've a Sunday-morning face of righteousness."

"What . . . ? Oh. Shall we go?"

"Waiting on you, that's all." They walked the acres of asphalt and found the elevator. "All right, DeFord, so you feel I'm not backing you up on this Raven business. Interesting."

"What?"

"Your dream, your dream. Oh my, DeFord, you may be the man of action on this little adventure of ours, but you're sadly mismatched in the introspective department." He punched a button, and the bottom fell from their feet. "While you've been chasing lions I've been chasing devils. But no more, no more. Let's get on with it. Sunday! Oh Lord, if He could only see what we've done to the day He once used for rest."

XIV

The mullet rolled, and this time DeFord saw its bluish back as it sank ogled-eyed to its spawning bed, a few tar-colored leeches clinging behind its carapaced head and among the warts of its leathery prehistoric skin.

"There!" Leggatt shouted to his ear. "See it now?"

The subway rails twisted, engine headlight careening at a wall of uprights before slipping free to roar straightway. Like a rigger Leggatt clung to the observation bar, shouting about subway rabbits, a phenomenon he had been shown by a pair of teen-age Puerto Rican male prostitutes one Sunday afternoon and for which he could offer no explanation. "Another! . . . black-tipped ears." Leggatt bellowed something about speed, the eyes' propensity to translate moving reflections—perhaps fluttering candy wrappers?—to a continuity.

But they were mullets. The prostitutes' image of magic white bunnies might dominate Leggatt's vision, but DeFord saw them as roiling mullets, those grotesque bottomfish which spawned each spring by the million from swampy Klamath Lake upwards into the Williamson River of eastern Oregon. For years he had driven the pass to snag mullet from the riverbed with his heaviest tackle, packing them in snow gathered at the crest and preserved with an inch of cedar sawdust gunnysacked at a shakemill en route. Then he trucked two or three hundred pounds to whatever town he was working out of and smoked fillets over sugary vine maple, planting the carcasses—each yet ten or fifteen pounds heavy with entrails, roe and warty cartilage—wherever he planned to set tomato plants.

"Fish, eh?" Leggatt shouted. "Anything's possible. What is most . . . everyone sees them . . . On the express between Ninety-sixth and Seventy-second—you can see a dozen . . . showed them to Codgers, but the old monkey saw . . . Yes, small naked adolescent girls . . . 'Rabbits?' he squealed. 'Nonsense! . . . No imagination, Johnie . . . If you insist a fertility symbol . . . but rabbits? Absurd!' "

God knows I wanted to help him—tried to, DeFord thought, almost before the next mullet appeared between the tracks, becoming Tanner, with eyes pointed upwards, wide to a sightless thousand caliber. His foreknowledge of the distortion frightened him more than the corpse, and he willed the prostitutes' innocent vision, only to have a rabbit—yes—next appear, but with a tightly rolled umbrella thrust ahead in a blindman's probe. Damn fool Tanner, he thought, damn damn fool. He stepped from the observation window and sat, dumbly registering that Leggatt remained balanced on his toes, studying the rabbits flushed from their concrete brush piles as if to make sense, order, art—yes, art—of the thing; guiltlessly picking for whatever joy or wonder. A remarkable man, Johnie. Maybe a great man even now at what? Thirty-five years. Well, he could accept that Leggatt had greatness—it did not make him feel less a man himself. What he had done since his thirties was done. That was all. The business with his heart had not changed how he felt about living; nor had meeting someone so ancient as Codgers; nor realizing that Leggatt's hunger made his own seem hardly hunger at all, more a dulled irritability. He had used his land, that was certain. Hunted, fished, worked, logged, harvested, built on it, walked most of it and seen most of the rest. But he had never used himself—except for whatever energy, interest or bullheadedness such things required. Truth was, he had been lucky. Fairly soon now, there would be damn little left about which a man could be as stubborn as he. Fairly soon now, people would have little but the amusements Leggatt's brother scrambled for all over town, or backyard hobbying in the new side-by-side shanties building up even as far north and west as where he had chosen to put his last place. Or if possible, to be a Leggatt—but he could not expect that . . . Yet, it was not for him to talk, as he had never used much of himself or of people and so was no hand to make predictions. This was old men's work, and he would be damned or dead before he got that old.

For the first time since leaving Craig, Colorado, he felt guilty. He had used and used and used, and thereby had lost knowledge of people like Tanner. Yes, it would be his fault if Tanner was dead, for all his use of things had made it next to impossible to learn how to understand a Tanner. He had always walked on, leaving the Tanners to pull for themselves. But what else? The question was: Does it work? A gyppo logger's byword, a brush engineer's measure, but after a bit, that was the question. Does it work? And if it doesn't, get what does up here so we can make bag. Well, he had thrown in with that brush morality. Does it work for you, Lyle? No? Then finish the chore, cash in and go down the road to something that does. Well damn, if he was guilty he had been lucky too. He would sure hate to start again with such a cedar butcher's twist. Yes, were he to be guilty for Tanner's suicide— Why had such an idea intruded anyway? Why was he so flat-assed certain Tanner had gone to the river? How could a man ever do such a thing? But were he guilty, it was not that his luck had soured. His luck simply wore out. Then what of Raven? How did Raven fit? Was Raven what happened if you always kept one hop in front of Leggatt's brother, that fellow Kreplun and that crowd in Greenwich Village? If he had mixed with their outfit, maybe Raven never would have meant a thing, never could have touched him, never even seen him. No, no, that had too ready a handle. That was not the way things turned.

As if plunged to its hubs in pumice, their subway ceased momentum long enough for them to gain the Union Square platform and watch it whet to silence. "That last . . . mullet you saw . . . didn't settle too well, it appears," said Leggatt, dropping his voice as they mounted the exit.

"I got to worrying, Tanner."

"For two days now, I've packed the idea you put a lot of work into what you've just called more dangerous. Now who could have put that in the back of my head?" DeFord said.

"Give me no high-country lip. Despite its treachery, I respect my incessant plucking at things. Although I treat it shabbily from—Ah, there's a friend."

The Negro from the Williamsburg Bridge urinal stood upon an egg crate, face aimed toward the sun above his bemused parishioners. "I saw God. Saw God with these sinful eyes. From the depths of my sin I saw God."

"What did she say?" Leggatt shouted.

" 'Johnie,' she say, 'give up your mary jane. Lay down your mary jane.' "

Leggatt steered DeFord toward Great Jones Street. "Why is it those who can see God either wrestle Him or get told off?"

Suddenly Raven's voice sought them. "There they-are! There-are the men I want-ed to rob. Ask-them if it is not-true!" Lower body painfully erect in his disheveled business suit, Joe Raven swayed on a bench, tears streaming down his cheeks. "Here is-the miracle of this-morning. The very people I want-ed to destroy could pass me-by and never know I-have-repented. Now-you see how this-could happen to you. And where then will you seek-help, having desired to ex-ploit your fellow-man?" He drew dirt from his pocket and sprinkled it over his head. "Three-steps to salvation. One, you re-cognize you have-wanted to sin. Two, you say: Joe, heap dirt up-on yourself and ask forgiveness. Three, you ask for help. Joe-Raven has sinned. Old-Man, do you forgive?"

"Forgive him," Leggatt prompted as a crowd firmed around them. "Play along till we see what Crook's up to."

DeFord nodded; Raven sobbed. "He-has forgiven! I tried to kill-him. I killed his-dog and tried to rob-him. Yet he-has forgiven. But Lord say wages of sin are-death. Yes. For when man sins-he is forgotten. Will-you forget Joe-Raven, who calls for your-help? Will you sin by forgetting Joe Raven, who vows-to sin no more? I-have sinned. I-have been forgiven. I need your-help." He poured more dirt, sobbing. "Give me your-help, that we can-prove we-are all buddies under God. Give-me your help that we-can start my life new, and I-shall come here each Sun-day to tell you-how I keep to the-Way and the-Truth. Give me your-help, and as you learn of my new life it-will inspire you too to say, 'I-have sinned, I ask for-giveness, I must have help.' " Crook and Proudhomme took off their hats and began circulating among the crowd. "Start believing by trust-ing. Put a few cents of your-hope into my hands to show-you want to believe, only a symbol of your-need to trust your fellow-man, to be buddies with God. I will-not betray you. I shall return next Sunday to tell you how your trust has been returned ten-fold. We do not need-a church. This bench is pul-pit enough. We can start our lives all-again." Crook shuffled blindly, beseechingly, with begging hat, as Leggatt pulled DeFord from the crowd and started them out of the square. All right, DeFord thought, I won't think about it. Not until I breakfast and get some rest.

◇ ◇ ◇

" 'Απο Θαγεῖ Θέλμ,' " squeaked Codgers. " 'I want to die.' So spake Sibyl of Cumae. Let me remind you: Sibyl, made love to by Zeus, is granted one wish. Picking a handful of sand, she asks for as many years as there are grains. She lives those grains but without youth, growing older, smaller, until nothing but a voice. A voice. She dwells in a bottle at the Cave of Cumae. Yet centuries of bodiless life bring great vision, so pilgrims journey to question the bottled Sibyl. Finally one asks what she wants. 'Απο Θαγεῖ Θέλμ.' I want to die."

DeFord had drawn a stool to Codgers' scrap barrel, and sitting over it, was working an edge to the broken tip of his pocketknife, tracing eights in a pumice of steel to whetstone.

Leggatt had described the night quite simply, summing up with: "So we couldn't find a job for DeFord, and I wasn't able to run down Frank, but we got the check back."

Codgers arranged their breakfast with deliberation: a large bunch of watercress, two sharp knives, half an onion, five eggs, milk, flour, cornstarch, salt, an egg whisk, three mixing bowls, saucepan, ceramic soufflé dish and a piece of lean pork. He passed one hairless parchment hand over this assemblage, then drew erect, bent double and brought forth from beneath his sink a large bottle of gin. This he thumped beside the pork, saying "Απο Θαγε͡ι Θέλμ," bemused.

"I remember. Silly-assed woman. Got what she deserved. And you left out the important part. It was Hera who realized Sibyl had asked for years, not youth, and cursed her. Zeus granted wisdom to compensate her aging. Not enough for hot-pants Sibyl; she wanted perpetual adolescence. History of her sex."

"Nonsense."

"You said yourself, 'I've been married six times, and never to the same woman.' Of anyone, you should know."

Codgers raised a hand and held it like a wand. "I accept. My point was Sibyl wanted to live life, not be cursed by it. My point is the myth applies to you." He hopped out of his kitchen, snatched Leggatt's coffee and prodded him toward the stove. "You once kept yourself alive as a short-order cook. We shall now make you a chef. You will create my Cantonese Watercress Soup Soufflé: a marriage of East and West conceived as a rebuttal to the most asinine of my contemporaries and developed—"

"Who?"

"Rudyard Kipling. And developed to assuage my appetite for watercress soup, at the same time binding the soup to something my stomach can hold long enough to derive some nourishment." Codgers squeaked an aside to DeFord: "My digestive machinery is not as young as that day I stopped in Brattleboro, Vermont, to see Kipling. Here, Johnie—you cut the cress into a paste."

"And the gin? Kipling's idea?" Leggatt stripped leaves

and pushed them to the dicing board with the back of his fingers.

"The gin," Codgers pronounced, snatching the knife from Leggatt, "is my own creation. And if you use two knives and no fingers instead of one knife and five fingers, you stand less chance of getting blood in my breakfast." He demonstrated, then squeezed farther into the kitchen, thrusting his head into the stove. "Although that would serve your particular sense of—" One ivory hand fumbled for the gas knob, the other struck a match.

"Extravagance," DeFord interjected, testing the edge of his blade and returning it to eights on the grindstone.

"Extravagance, Mr. DeFord?" Codgers' head reappeared as his hand found the gas and twisted. He knelt by the stove amidst the hiss, holding the lighted match and staring at DeFord. "Do not use the word lightly. Lately I am making allowances for the seemingly irrational—extravagant as it may seem. Never underestimate the irrational, Mr. DeFord. When I was younger, I took great pleasure in finding all about me that which was rational, honorable, good. Now I see in everything the irrational, the cruel, the evil. Extravagance, yes. Johnie's life and my life will always be extravagant."

"I'll admit I've never seen such a man as Johnie for crowding things around his head."

Codgers turned again to his stove, lighting his way with the match. "The word is 'indulging,' Mr. DeFord."

WHA-UMPH-PAA!

"Jesus Christ!"

Leggatt leapt to wrap the old man's smoldering turtleneck in a damp cloth.

"Separate five eggs and beat their yolks until frothy. But no more! We don't want them tough. Rubbery. For me there is little heat to anything any more. Must be how the lower animals feel when they're ready for hibernation. Man should relearn to hibernate. But his nature disavows it. Something Johnie has not yet learned. In his effort to repair himself Johnie accepted the pain of thinking, and now he's hibernating with that pain. It has become a friend."

"Why, you old mummer." Leggatt broke eggs and carefully passed yolks from shell half to shell half, separating. "How can you sit there pronouncing like a tarot card?"

"Don't be trivial. My intellection is the fourth after three lives of association. So it is fitting I can devote myself to it, as I already have outlived the rest. Albeit the urges to engage, to procreate."

"The urge to procreate?"

"You look shocked."

"Good Christ! How old must you be before—"

"You no longer want to procreate?" Codgers' face exploded with wrinkles. "You'll have to ask someone older than I, Johnie."

"I find it impossible to believe you."

Codgers stared, pouted, then cleared his throat. "I think you had best leave my kitchen."

"All right." Leggatt pitched eggshells between DeFord's hands and into the scrap barrel. "No offense. No offense. I'll listen . . . go on."

"Business first." Codgers stirred milk, flour, salt, a teaspoon of onion juice in a saucepan and carefully heated it. "When this thickens, take it from the heat and add a bit of the beaten yolk— Don't stand there looking sheepish. Beat the yolk! You must stir the bit of yolk into the sauce in order to cool it sufficiently so it will not congeal the remainder of the yolks . . . Don't bruise them. That's it, gently." He scraped up the watercress paste and brought it to DeFord upon the flat of a knife.

Ah yes, DeFord thought, closing his eyes and smelling of it. Codgers faced him over the knife blade of cress. "You must come and visit me," DeFord found himself saying. "You must come and stay with me, Mr. Codgers. I have watercress in my stream, and chickens I've fenced on a hillside. I feed them cracked corn, and they range on their own."

"Yes. Yes." Codgers pranced back to his kitchen and mixed the cress paste in the sauce and egg yolks. "I've eaten such eggs. So fresh their yolks stand on a pan as if solid. Here—beat the whites now. I no longer have the wrist for it." He watched, seemed satisfied, turned to DeFord. "When will you leave? What did your doctor say?"

DeFord shrugged. He was not sure. He could go now, he supposed, any time. It was only . . . Raven, he supposed. He would still like to talk with Raven.

Codgers said nothing, simply folded his hands in his lap and regarded them, nodding pleasurably when Leggatt grunted with his work. "So," he pronounced finally. "So you insist this land is big enough for even Joe Raven? Well, you're wrong, Mr. DeFord. It's not even big enough for you. No. No. There should be new frontiers for men like you. We should stamp your image upon our nickels in place of the buffalo and give you fresh frontiers where you can bury yourself and try again. And Leggatt with you."

"I'm doing all right, thank you," said Leggatt. "And just how long do you want these damn things beaten, anyway?"

"Until stiff. But not dry. Until they come up in little hills when you pull the whisk from them. So you missed him, eh?"

"Who?"

"Frank. He left just before you arrived. Said he looked

for you most of last night. But I think he was lying. Another advantage of great age. You can smell a lie al—"

"Well, Jesus Christ! Why didn't you tell me?"

"I was hungry. I do have my appetites, you know. I was afraid you'd go off before breakfasting."

"Where's my money?"

"Frank has it with him. Wants to talk with you. He'll be at his girl's place all morning. He left her address." Codgers pointed. Leggatt searched, moved the gin bottle and found the address. "Gin! We have yet to make a sauce." Codgers minced lean pork and cress stems. "Now just before the soufflé comes from its oven we'll cook and strain this, add a tablespoon of cornstarch and a suspicion of gin. Then we'll pour it over the soufflé."

DeFord came barefoot from the bathroom and started to put on a pair of socks.

"How far do we have to go, Johnie?"

"Off lower Fifth. Right back where we started. Fuck it. I'm in no mood to meet his latest discovery. Crazy broads. He likes them dumb and busty."

"That's not much of a hike. You've time to shave, shit and saddle before breakfast." DeFord relaced his boots. "I've a built-in timer too."

"I mean it, DeFord. I'm tired of running about, trying to grab a few hundred bucks from my brother's floating crap game. I climbed that goddamn ladder yesterday, and that's all I have to do. Those money-grubbing bastard friends of Frank's and Frank-him-fucking-self can shove their patronage. I'll go back to selling shoes at—"

"Silence," squeaked Codgers. "My soufflé! It's rising now. Your ridiculous, prideful, incessant thinking, your nonsense will ruin—

"Nonsense?"

"Nonsense. Johnie, you know this. Your life is full of conflict, dissociation, moral intolerance, anger. You are using abstractions yourself in your efforts to escape sterility, and it's castrating you. Stop thinking! Live life! Take Frank's money! Paint! Go winter with DeFord! Marry a muse! Exhibit next spring!"

"What! To prove your goddamn theories?"

"Don't be trivial. Now shave, shower and whatever."

"Trivial?" Leggatt called.

"Trivial. I met you the day you became an Elizabeth Street man. I was present the very day you moved under the shadow of the bridge to commence your kill or cure. The discipline of your work has completed your metamorphosis. The only thing that remains is to lay aside the very abstractions that saved you, as now they have become unnecessary. For the man you are now, your intellectual life is trivial, because as with all trivial things, you find it comfortable and adequate." Codgers crept back to his kitchen and winked to DeFord. "It's taken me one hundred and seven years to be able to say that. And see the results? Silence. Yet to silence Johnie is a reward of sorts."

"So it has come to this," Leggatt yelled. "Lured by a gourmand's breakfast, I'm spoon-fed solutions."

"Solutions? If you want solutions, then begin at once your autobiography. Omit not one detail. As you record the last act of the last moment you will be recording the last solution. The great secret is to one day break the chain. Start afresh."

"You are asking for total rebirth."

"I ask for nothing. I was a professor—of philosophy, as a matter of fact—professors do not ask. They offer and see who is hungry."

Leggatt, at last, remained silent.

DeFord held his knife poised, thumb testing its edge, lips pursed, thinking: To break the chain, to start again, fresh.

And Codgers laid their plates, tiptoeing about his stove,

humming. "It has not fallen. I sense it is still with us, Mr. DeFord," he whispered.

"What?" Under his thumb his knife was edged again, sharp as ever, but with its tip gone, its balance was gone too. He closed it into his palm and put it to rest in his pocket.

"My soufflé. Made it through." He gestured at the bathroom. "Survived. I can sense it. You know, Mr. DeFord, I love that boy." He brought his face close to DeFord's. "All my sons . . . grew up to become—would you pardon a very dated expression?—they became American bourgeois. Cursed. Respectable. Dull. Common as dirt. But righteous, oh yes. I provided for them very well, but all they grew up to respect was the providing. You'd have thought one of them might have wanted to do something. Risk himself. But they were cowards, Mr. DeFord." Codgers made his eyes go round as a child's. "Our land is millioned with them. It is the curse of America. But I love my country. Oh yes. I've seen it all. Forty years ago I saw it all. Tell me, has it changed much, really?"

"Yes." DeFord shook his head. "Yes, but not really. No. Not really. Not yet. Not quite yet."

"There is room enough then for Johnie. I was wrong. Good. I do love that boy. He's absolutely insane, that boy. Oh, he's a man, Mr. DeFord."

"SOS," Leggatt called, coming from his shower, combing his hair with his fingers. "AC-DC. DOA. AWOL. Where's my grub?"

"Everyone to his seat. Fork in hand." Codgers drew on two huge insulated mittens. "It will be beautiful, brown as a wild mushroom, and perfectly, perfectly light. It will be a remarkable breakfast. Remarkable."

◇ ◇ ◇

"Frank's at church," Frank's girl announced through a crack between door and jamb exactly the width of one sky-blue eye.

Into the skeptical chatter of parakeets Leggatt explained.

"Oh. So you're Frank's brother? I'd like so to 'vite you in, but Frank makes me keep the police chain on since that woman—you know in Brooklyn?—was stabbed through her peekhole."

If Frank had left an envelope, perhaps. Or mentioned some money.

"Frank just jumped up of a sudden and said he's going to church. Always business with Frank."

Yes, Leggatt understood. But had Frank left any money? Or a message? Had his brother mentioned just what church?

Leggatt asked, very, very slowly, just when the hell Frank said he'd be back.

"He didn't. He just said he would go by himself. Walk."

◇ ◇ ◇

"Re-pent!" Joe Raven shouted. "Repent, forgive, help. There are my buddies I-would have hurt. Here is the money I-took from them." Raven passed DeFord's worthless checks among his listeners and bade them examine. As Leggatt and DeFord drew near he tore them to confetti, heaping the top of his head. "We-have all sinned. This old-man, what sins does he-carry? Who had he turned-his back to in-need? Will he atone-now by helping me who sin-ned against him?" He moved quickly after DeFord. "John-nie. Old-man. Wait." He scraped confetti from his hair. "Your-checks. You see. I have re-pented."

"You know damn well those were worthless."

"Ahh, John-nie." Raven dragged thighs furiously to

remain abreast. "You spoil-it. I-knew. That is-not what I repent." He struggled upright, wiping the spittle of his effort on his sleeve. "I re-pent for Jaxon Tanner . . . Ahh, old-man. You stop now."

"Ignore him, DeFord. The longer we listen, the quicker Crook and Alfred will be back from the nearest Sunday bootlegger."

"He-wants to hear, John-nie. Wants to hear how I met-his buddy last night while looking for-you. Wants to hear how his bud-dy asked me for-help before he went to the river. Maybe he will-find it amus-sing Tanner asked-me for help. That-is what-I-repent. That I did-not help poor-Tanner. But he was not my bud-dy. I-thought he was your-buddy, old-man."

The loud habit of his heart rose to DeFord's ears, and he knew he must rest, if only a few moments. His fatigue had so deepened it frightened him, for in the place where he should expect the pain of remorse there beat on the habit of his heart. He feared for himself, feared what he might do.

"Per-haps you do not believe. We can prove-it. Crook and Al-fred have gone-for the paper."

DeFord moved away. "I'll take that when it comes."

"Stink-king old-man! When it comes? I tell-you when it-comes! It-comes every day. I'll be with-you every-day until you repent. You won't be-free until you-repent. You hear me, stink-king old man?"

They outdistanced Raven. So Tanner needed me sorely, after all? Well, I shall not run. But let it come tomorrow, after a rest. Then let it come. Leggatt motioned and they entered a church, sitting apart from the worshipers. DeFord listened to the intonations of robed priests, moving in slow circles, apparently tied forever to a rusty feeder chain whose gears ground eternally in some secret sub-cellar far below the altar. He swallowed two pills, closed his eyes and had been resting perhaps five, perhaps fifteen minutes when something, some movement, startled him.

A piece of paper fluttered to his lap, a hand withdrew and DeFord, blinking, watched a small man retreat through the open church doors.

Memo: Your room full of police and the bosses who do not wear uniforms.

Hurrying after Leggatt, who had followed the small man, DeFord found them huddled together, Johnie clasping the arm of a baggy suit.

"Dee Bee, what in God's name is this?"

The little man's eyes closed. "Dee Bee Smith. Ah, he . . . saw you and wanted"—his eyes widened upon DeFord—"to tell him about the police. He gave Dee Bee a favor."

Leggatt loosened his grip. "I see. I see. Tell me, why did Dee Bee send you?"

"Dee Bee is looking . . . a new block. He saw you and got off bus. Then sent me. But he has gone onto new block. No one knows where."

"Ah, that's a shame. I would have wanted to say goodbye. We wanted to wish Dee Bee luck. He was an old friend. For a minute I thought you were the Dee Bee I knew. But the Dee Bee I knew seemed much more content, happy."

The man drew closer. "Memo: Dee Bee Smith will be his old self. When disguise gets worn and comfortable."

"I'm glad. But what's this note?"

"He . . . uh, wanted you to know Tanner—you helped last night—is dead. Police and They came to his room just as Dee Bee went to bring . . . something. They said he had been pushed or killed himself. They said."

"And what does Dee Bee think?"

"Hee hee. Memo: Tanner had no disguise, so he jumped into the river."

Ahhh, thought DeFord. So I have killed him. He slipped down the wall to a stair while the priest's voice sounded in the public-address system feeding the classroom below. Killed him, then. Might as well have pushed him. The damn, damn fool. No. No! I shall not take responsibility for this. I shall not let it keep me in this city. I shall return to my house. I shall not fail.

"I'm rested now," DeFord said. "Let's get on with it." They climbed the stairs.

◇ ◇ ◇

"Look, DeFord, we're both tired. Let's forget the money."

"No." They were walking east from Sixth to Fifth now, Raven behind them. Whenever DeFord stopped, Raven would halt and wave the morning's paper, drawing pedestrians to his cause. Sighting along Raven's paper, the curious stared ahead to where DeFord stood watching. Then DeFord would walk on. He would find Frank for Johnie —there was still a chance. Had not the girl said a church nearby? Perhaps they would be lucky. Luck bunched like habit, and since their luck had run so foul, it might be due for a change. Perhaps Frank Leggatt could be found and half the job busheled. He knew now what he had sensed ever since Leggatt swung over the Williamsburg Bridge railing: Leggatt existed from one winter's stake to the next and doubtless would forever run that way, whether or not he exhibited at every capital in the States. And he, DeFord, existed from one chore to the next and would be doing so the hour his heart gave out. It was a bean picker's way. And so he knew Leggatt would keep after his brother because the bean picker in him knew damn well you had to bushel at least half your contract or you were off to nowhere in a bucket.

He consoled himself with this. Yet he still avoided the

truth—that in recognizing Raven's habit of stopping each time DeFord stopped, like an antelope being stalked, he knew how to rid himself of Raven.

They passed onto Fifth Avenue as if crossing a watershed into country so truly different DeFord looked back to check his path. Raven still followed, trailing like some bundle of towed rags.

The three of them moved among the rich, between curbed limousines, and uniformed doormen, all the while Leggatt studied the pavement until he blurted out to no one in particular, "All right, I must paint through this winter, that's certain. So I might as well get the money from one son of a bitch as another."

"At least it's in the family."

"You're full of balls this morning, aren't you?"

"I am a bit skookum." Yet DeFord's body denied it even as he spoke. He stopped, checked Raven, and yes, the damn fool had frozen motionless.

Perhaps it was that he knew suddenly Raven was hanging on as desperately as he, that Raven had had no whiskey for six hours, that Raven had been worn to nothing but hate—in short, Raven was human. Perhaps that was it.

Perhaps he realized that even if they found Frank Leggatt it was no guarantee Leggatt would winter with him —maybe less, since Leggatt would have his own stake. And although DeFord had retrieved his check, he had not been able to stop Raven, so it seemed a DeFord had lost again.

Perhaps it was only that his heart understood the thing his principles—his own *Carpenter's Manual* or whatever anyone might choose to hang a name to—did not admit: remorse and guilt were less oppressive than fear.

Perhaps it was that in the moments between Leggatt's saying, "There's the ethical-culture place, and damn if there isn't Frank ethical-culting his way to his car!" and the instant Raven disappeared beneath three tons of Rolls Royce in a scream of brakes, horns and churchgoers—in those moments he accepted what would happen, welcoming it as the something he had needed all his life, the something he owed the land he used, the payment without which his place in Oregon would never be truly his whether he lived to return or not.

Whatever, he allowed it: gauging the threat of the heavy limousines, that jerked impatiently toward the changing traffic light; allowed and welcomed the sudden, almost erotic anticipation.

Allowed, welcomed and hated all in the same instant in which Raven—motionless because he, DeFord, had frozen just safely beyond the wall of now alert and frantically braking limousines—suddenly knew and opened his mouth to scream.

It was Mr. Nicholas who parted the crowd, called the attending police by first name, commandered Leggatt and Deford to his car and drove them away from the howling pain of Raven. Mr. Nicholas had had a marvelous, perfect Sunday and was on his way to Mass, having, he hinted, just seen his nephew Victor, who was yet a bit white around the eyes, do a wonderful piece of rather nasty work: the kind of work Mr. Nicholas always preferred to do on Sunday, just before Mass. Mr. Nicholas saved all his bad jobs for Sunday. Sunday had always been his lucky day.

◇ ◇ ◇

Dee Bee Smith watches Johnie and the old lumberman walk under the door arch and leave the church. Everyone is on his knees. The priest intones, and They answer from their knees. Dee Bee strokes his silk, thinking: I am free now and it was better about package. He moves where the great cathedral itself relinquishes and reclaims its vaulted breath. Yes, it was better about package, Dee Bee repeats, remembering mounting the stairs to the old lumberman's room—police all around him, and they had drawn him, afraid and itching beneath his clean underwear, into Tanner's room. But it was only Tanner who interested them—although one policeman ran after him to return package when he left it there on Tanner's bed. That was the worst part. When Pearshape approached, it had been the easiest—punching a hole in package with a piece of bottle and leading Pearshape along the trail of white powder down the alley and into the basement, where he threw the rest into the hot-water furnace and slipped out his secret way, pursued only by the screams issuing from Pearshape's direction. The strength he received from that stricken animal cry urged him on to the bus, to pay the driver and slip into a seat, where he did not once look back upon block. For he had defeated Them. Defeated Them forever. They would never again send their spies to seek him out, to seek out Dee Bee Smith alone of all the others and turn him back from his way to responsibility and whiskey.

ABOUT THE AUTHOR

After attending both Cornell and Columbia universities, David Shetzline worked as a truck driver, short-order cook, Forest Service Lookout and surveyor's aid. Thirty-one years of age, he now lives with his wife and three children on a small ranch south of Portland, Oregon.